The Eagle Tree

Through the magical talents of the Wizard Lucifer John McCracken, Prince Pugnax of Porzana
has been turned into a giant cockroach! And, to
tell the truth, his subjects are not too upset about
it. Until they hear about his nephew Bembex,
who is about to take over. His plans for 'devel-
oping' their forest are not popular at all – maybe
old Pugnax was not so bad after all? Can they get
him back – in human form?

DAN KISSANE

Dan lives on a farm in Kerry where he keeps sheep and bees. His first book *The King of Wisdom's Daughter* was published in 1995. This, his second, follows the same characters in another wild and wonderful adventure.

The Eagle Tree

DAN KISSANE

Illustrations

Aileen Johnston

THE O'BRIEN PRESS

DUBLIN

First published 1996 by The O'Brien Press Ltd.
20 Victoria Road, Dublin 6, Ireland

British Library Cataloguing-in-publication Data
A catalogue reference for this title is available from the British Library.

ISBN 0-86278-486-7

1 2 3 4 5 6 7 8 9 10
96 97 98 99 00 01 02 03 04 05 06

The O'Brien Press receives assistance from
The Arts Council/An Chomhairle Ealaíon

Typesetting, layout, design: The O'Brien Press Lrd.
Cover illustration: Aileen Johnston
Printing: Cox & Wyman Ltd.

Lucifer John McCracken, setter of bones, maker of charms, gatherer of herbs, gazer at stars and caster of spells, sat on an upside-down butter-box outside his cottage door and stared up at the night sky. For an hour he gazed at the great constellation of Orion which arose in glory from behind the southern mountains. He watched until Sirius, the Dog Star, which follows at Orion's heel, appeared above the horizon, and his eyes began to twinkle merrily in a perfect reflection of that star's own twinkling. 'There you are at last!' he said quietly. 'I was beginning to think you weren't coming tonight.'

He shifted his gaze north across the heavens, and his eyes came to rest on the Plough, and particularly on the tiny star in its tail which shows itself only on perfectly clear nights. A faint smile came to his lips: he had been watching that very star on just such a night as this twelve months ago. That was the night when Pugnax, Prince of Porzana, and Atin Bush, the Magician of Coil, had come with a hare's ear and what they thought was a raven's quill to strip him of his magic powers. Unfortunately for them, their spell had backfired, turning them both into giant cockroaches.

Lucifer John had since heard that in Atin Bush's case the spell had worn off – probably because he had been second to suffer it and the charms had by then lost much of their potency. But poor old Pugnax ... well, it wasn't Lucifer John's problem. As these thoughts came to him, a falling star flashed through the firmament. 'That means something,' said the old wizard to himself, with a slight prickly feeling at the back of his neck. 'I wonder what ...?'

PART 1

CHAPTER 1

BREAKFAST IN BELLONIA

Bembex, Baron of Bellonia, knocked the top off his egg, inspected the contents with a critical eye and shuddered. Flinging down his egg-spoon in disgust, he shoved his chair away from the polished oak table, threw back his head and shouted at the top of his voice: 'Parker! Parker!'

He paused, listened attentively, and then shouted again, even louder: 'Parker! PARKER! PAAAR-KERRR!!!' This second summons proved no more fruitful than the first, and he was about to give tongue again when the door of the breakfast-room opened and an elderly, grey-haired man dressed in a butler's uniform glided in.

'You called, sir?' he said in a toneless voice.

'I did indeed, Parker,' said the Baron irritably. 'What's the meaning of this? My egg is overboiled again! In fact,' he continued, 'you could hardly call it an egg. It's a bullet! Understand? Bullet! And I won't have it, d'you hear?'

The butler's face betrayed no emotion. 'Very good, sir.'

'Very good?' repeated Bembex, in an astonished voice. 'Very *good*? It's not very good, Parker! It's quite the opposite! Sack the cook!' he cried. 'Turn her out, bag and baggage! I've warned her about this before!'

The butler looked as though he was about to sigh, but contented himself with a cough instead. 'The cook resigned yesterday, sir,' he said blandly. 'She said something about non-payment of wages. Your breakfast was prepared this morning by the gardener.'

Bembex gaped. 'The gardener? Cooking my breakfast?' He eyed the egg suspiciously as if he half-expected it to sprout leaves. 'That explains it! Cooking, according to my way of looking at things, is supposed to be done by cooks! The proper occupation for gardeners is gardening. Tell him to mind his own business in the future.'

'That will not be necessary, sir. After eating his own

breakfast, the gardener also gave notice and left.'

Bembex ground his teeth. 'Swine!' he breathed. 'Just because of a temporary cash-flow problem they desert me like rats leaving a sinking ship. What's the world coming to, Parker? People take no pride in their positions any more. All we hear nowadays is "Money, money, money!" It's nothing more than one long struggle from cradle to grave to gather up as much of the filthy lucre as possible. Don't you agree, Parker?'

The butler confined his answer to a slight lifting of the eyebrows. He stepped forward and picked up the egg. 'Since this has proved unacceptable, sir, it may come in useful elsewhere.'

'Oh, help yourself, Parker,' said the baron morosely. 'Don't mind me – I'm only the lord and master of the place. It doesn't matter if I starve!' He gave a little sniff. 'What's for lunch?'

'Sardine, sir.'

'Sardines? Is that all?'

'Not sardines, sir, sardine: there's only one left. The gardener ate the rest before he departed.'

Bembex banged his fist on the table. 'Greedy swine!' he cried. 'If I had any wages to give him I'd deduct the price of them!'

Parker crossed to the door and paused as he opened it. 'One other thing, sir. There is a gentleman to see you.

Shall I show him in?'

'Gentleman?' said Bembex warily. People known to him who could be called 'gentlemen' were few and far between, and those who could were unlikely to pay social calls at breakfast-time. 'To see me?' he said. 'What sort of gentleman?'

'He gave his name as a Mr Scolopax, sir. I believe he is a solicitor.'

Bembex's jaw dropped. 'Solicitor!' he hissed. He didn't like the sound of this. Solicitors, in the Baron's experience, usually came armed with writs which demanded instant payment of long-overdue bills, and with promises of terrible punishments in the event of non-payment. 'Get rid of him, Parker. Tell him I've gone to Jamaica or that I'm dead or something.'

The butler gave a little cough. 'Knowing your aversion to callers of the type, sir, I offered the first-mentioned explanation, but the gentleman responded that he would sit in the hall and await your return. Like all lawyers, he apparently accepts nothing without proof. Were I to tell him of your death, sir, he might well ask to see the corpse.'

Bembex chewed his lower lip and considered. 'Oh, all right, Parker. You'd better show him in.'

The old man whom Parker ushered into the breakfast-room and announced as Mr Scolopax had a distinct air of solemnity about him. His clothes were solemn, his manner was solemn, and, most of all, his expression was solemn. He looked like he had never entertained a silly thought or idea in his life and had no intention of doing so now. Bembex eyed him nervously. These lawyers were not to be trusted; the only way to deal with them was to forestall them and deny everything.

'Ah!' he said, smiling brightly. 'Scolopax! Do come in and sit down. I can explain everything.'

The lawyer took a seat and looked at the baron with raised eyebrows. 'I beg your pardon, Baron,' he said.

'Er ...' said Bembex, still smiling. 'I mean to say ... it's all a mistake. It can easily be put right. Would you care for a bit of toast?' he added, waving a half-eaten slice in the air.

'Do you mean to tell me,' said the lawyer, sitting forward on the edge of his chair, 'that you know where he is?'

'Eh?' said Bembex. He paused, considering. 'Well, of course I know where a lot of chaps are ... perhaps you could be a bit more specific. Who exactly do you mean?'

'Mean?' echoed Mr Scolopax. 'Why, his Highness, of course. Who else could I mean?'

'Of course, of course,' said Bembex in a flurry, his mind racing. And then: 'Ah ... which Highness was that again?'

'Why, Pugnax of course, the Prince of Porzana – your uncle!'

'Old Uncle Puggy?' cried Bembex, immensely relieved that he himself was not the subject of this interview. 'Is that what this is all about? What's he done?'

'Are you not aware, Baron, that the Prince has not been seen for the past twelve months? Repeated enquiries have been unable to find out his whereabouts.'

'You don't say? You mean he's done a bunk?'

Here the lawyer looked a little uncomfortable. 'Rumour has it, Baron,' he began, 'and I stress that it is merely rumour – a ridiculous story in my opinion – that he was turned into a ... into a cockroach by some kind of a wizard, Lucifer John McSomething or other – Bracken or Fracken – I can't remember now.'

'What?' spluttered Bembex, laughing. 'Uncle Puggy? Turned into a cockroach? By a wizard? Of course,' he added with a chuckle, 'it wouldn't be a very hard job; I mean, old Pugnax was half way there as it was!'

Mr Scolopax frowned and looked solemn. 'As I said, Baron, it is merely a rumour. But the fact of the matter is that the prince has been officially missing since this time last year.'

'Well? What's it got to do with me? I haven't got him. You can search if you like!'

Scolopax shook his head. 'Baron, let me explain. I

represent the Porzana estate. If your uncle has not returned by twelve o'clock tomorrow night, you, as his only living relative, are the new owner of Porzana Castle and all that goes with it.'

Bembex sat motionless while he digested this. Then, trembling with excitement, he said: 'How much was the old goat worth?'

'I beg your pardon?' said Scolopax haughtily.

'How much was he worth? How much did he leave?'

The lawyer stared at Bembex for a moment; then, fishing a piece of paper out of his briefcase, he examined it critically before saying: 'When everything is added up, all debts called in, all accounts settled, including my own (which is very reasonable), the Porzana estate is worth precisely ah ...' he glanced again at the paper, looked up, blinked at the baron and said: 'nothing.'

Bembex leaped to his feet. 'Nothing?' he cried. '*Nothing*? D'you mean to say you came all the way out here to tell me I've inherited nothing? What's the good of becoming Prince of Porzana if there's nothing in it? I might just as well become a ... a ... a gardener!'

The solicitor shrugged. 'Well, of course, there's the title, the prestige ...'

Bembex stared at Scolopax as though the lawyer were something he wouldn't wish to step on with his new shoes.

But Scolopax was unmoved: lawyers are like that, they have thick skins which are proof against offended glances and injured stares. 'Of course,' he said encouragingly, 'there are the grounds: a lot of mature woodland, valuable stands of timber ...'

'Trees?' said Bembex hopefully. 'That's more like it! How many trees?'

Scolopax shook his head. 'Off-hand, I couldn't say, but a fair amount. Certainly more than ten acres.'

'Well,' said Bembex, 'that sounds encouraging. I had a lot of trees here in Bellonia once. Cut 'em all down and sold 'em to a paper mill. Maybe I could do the same again. Anything else there?' he added. 'Servants? Livestock? I seem to remember that Uncle Puggy used to go in for a bit of farming – sheep, hens, cattle and so on.'

Scolopax nodded. 'That's correct. But the servants had to fend for themselves when the Prince disappeared and, unfortunately, they transformed the sheep into mutton, the hens into chicken and the cows into beef. And when all that was gone, they themselves disappeared.' Here the lawyer consulted his notes again. 'Apart from the gardener,' he continued. 'Jacob Stobbins, the only remaining servant.'

With that, the solicitor replaced his papers in his briefcase and stood up, indicating that the interview was over. 'You'll be hearing from me in due course, Baron,' he said with a slight bow, and, walking to the door, he let himself out.

When he had gone, Bembex paced up and down, his head shrunk into his shoulders, his hands clasped behind his back. After a moment, Parker reappeared. 'Is there anything I can get you, sir?'

Bembex considered. 'Yes, Parker, there is. Bring in that sardine. I think I'll have it now.'

CHAPTER 2

NO PICNIC FOR PUGNAX

Pugnax, one-time prince of Porzana, was not a happy man. In fact, to be more precise, he was not a man at all. If you have read a book called *The King of Wisdom's Daughter* you will know that, following an encounter with the wizard Lucifer John McCracken, he had ended up in the shape of a giant cockroach. Ever since, he had been spending his time wandering around in the forest, feeling sorry for himself and ... well ... just being a cockroach.

Now you might be under the impression that being a cockroach is rather fun – no work, no school, nobody telling you what to do and nobody telling you what *not* to do. However, Pugnax had examined the situation from the inside out and the conclusion he had arrived at was: *Being a cockroach is definitely not fun!*

First of all, consider the question of diet: as a cockroach, all you get to eat is various kinds of food which can be broadly grouped together under the heading of *rubbish*. This can be almost anything, such as crumbs from stale cheese sandwiches, bits of castaway apple cores, segments of mouldy oranges, bits of rotten bananas, and other unpleasant things which would be too disgusting to mention here.

Secondly, just look at the company with which a cockroach is forced to associate: earwigs, woodlice, beetles, centipedes and, of course, other cockroaches – in short, every type of low-life imaginable! And if you've ever tried to hold an intelligent conversation with an earwig ... well, just try it the next time you see one and let me know how you get on!

And thirdly, I don't know whether you've ever noticed, but a cockroach's skin is not exactly the most comfortable thing to spend the day strolling around in. It's made out of very hard leathery stuff and is extremely tight-fitting, with bits sticking in here and other bits sticking out there, and the poor cockroach is all cramped up inside and can't stretch or scratch himself or do any of the other things that make life worth living. Is it any wonder that cockroaches are generally down in the dumps?

On top of all this, and I really don't like to speak badly of poor Pugnax because it's like kicking a man when he's down or throwing water on a drowned rat, but when he was a human being (if that is not too flattering a description of what he was before he gained insect status) Pugnax had a very unpleasant habit of picking his nose on every possible occasion. Of course, once he became a cockroach, that was out. Cockroaches do not have noses for a start, and even if they did, they don't have any fingers to poke into them, a serious matter for a dedicated nose-picker.

From all this, you can easily understand why Pugnax, as he wandered around the forest, was far from happy with his lot. He would think of days gone by and of how he had lived it up when he was a prince, lording it over his minions, eating and drinking the best of everything and generally having a good time, and he would sigh. And when he remembered how Lucifer John McCracken had tricked him into changing himself into a cockroach, he would groan.

One fine morning, feeling even more depressed than usual, Pugnax was wandering listlessly through the forest, sighing and groaning, when there came to his ears the unmistakeable sounds of merriment: peals of laughter, shouts of excitement and much loud talk. During the last year, Pugnax had gathered a great knowledge of the forest and its environs and he was immediately able to pinpoint the source of these sounds. They came from the small lake which nestled in the very centre of the wood.

He decided to investigate. His antennae quivering with excitement, he made his way there, picking his steps carefully through the trees, making as little noise as possible.

The side of the lake which he approached was fringed by a thick bed of bulrushes, their silvery tassels waving in the breeze. Silently he forced his way through until he reached the water's edge, getting his feet uncomfortably wet in the process. Keeping himself hidden behind a clump of kingcups, he peered out at the scene before him. A party of revellers had chosen the little lake as the venue for a bathing party. Men and women dressed in colourful bathing suits cavorted merrily, splashing water at each other, disappearing beneath the surface and then leaping up, all the time trading jokes and shrieking with laughter.

Pugnax himself had never been able to understand the attraction of throwing oneself into water. Water, in his opinion, was fine for boiling potatoes or mixing through whiskey, but when one came into bodily contact with it, it was always so disagreeably wet. However, there was no doubt about it – these people were

definitely enjoying it. That fact alone grated on Pugnax's nerves. 'Dirty rotten stinkers!' he muttered under his breath. 'Carrying on like that when a man of my calibre has to skulk around in the bulrushes in the form of a cockroach.'

He cast an eye along the bank of the lake, and there, not twenty yards from where he lay hidden, he beheld an object which caused him to quiver from one end of his body to the other – nothing more nor less than a large picnic basket. Obviously the bathing party had decided to make a day of it and have a lakeside lunch.

Pugnax was fond of picnic baskets. As Prince of Porzana, his idea of a high time had been to sit on the lawn on a sunny day with a well-filled hamper and little (or no) company. Visions of cold roast chicken, hard-boiled eggs and bottles of chilled beer floated before his eyes, and he came to a momentous decision. One can have enough of anything, and Pugnax now realised that he had had enough, and more than enough, of being a cockroach. 'I won't stand for it any longer!' he said aloud. 'The spirits of my noble ancestors won't put up with it! Am I not Pugnax, Prince of Porzana? A member of one of the most noble dynasties in the land? A family whose very name is synonymous with courage, fidelity, honour, uprightness and honesty? I am! And I will regain my birthright! But first I must sneak over and pinch that picnic basket ...'

Putting himself into reverse, he backed away from the lake until he was safely hidden from view. Then, forcing a new path through the bulrushes, he travelled along parallel to the water's edge until he reached the point where he judged the picnic basket lay. Turning once more towards the waterside, he surprised two wild duck who took to the air with a tremendous quacking. Pugnax ducked down, his heart pounding in his chest like a tennis ball. But the bathers hadn't noticed, for when Pugnax came to the edge of the bulrushes and peered out, fearful that he had been spotted, he was relieved to see that the swimmers were still splashing and laughing and cavorting. And better still, the picnic basket lay only a few feet away!

He summoned up all his courage, waited until all the bathers were at the far side of the little lake, then leaped wildly from his cover and rushed across the last few feet. Grasping the basket by one handle, he dragged it back into the rushes. Fear of capture lending him strength, he hoisted it onto his back and ran off, staggering under the weight, expecting every moment to hear cries of 'Hey you!' or 'Stop! Thief!'

But no such cries came to his ears and before long, he was once more concealed in the safety of the forest.

When he had put what he considered a safe distance

between himself and the little lake, he stopped in a shady clearing. Gasping, he slid the basket off his back, placed it gently on the ground and stared at it with glee. He unfastened the little clasp which secured the lid, a dribble of saliva running from the corner of his mouth at the thought of the contents. He could almost taste the roasted chicken – the brown crackly skin, the succulent white flesh – and the thought of the sharp, sparkling beer almost made him cry!

Imagine then his feelings, the depth of his disappointment, when, on flinging back the lid, instead of the tasty delights he had expected he beheld nothing more than an assorted jumble of socks, shoes, underwear, bath towels and other items of clothing!

With a groan which worked its way up from the bottom of his soul, he sank to the ground, his mouth open in disbelief.

'Oh!' he said in a small, hurt voice. 'How could they?' Then, jumping to his feet, he began to kick the basket up and down the clearing, scattering garments this way and that.

'Dirty, rotten, stinking, treacherous rotters!' he raged. 'Guttersnipes! Assassins! There ought to be a law against it! Leading a fellow to believe he's going to get chicken and beer and then fobbing him off with smelly socks and folderols! Dirty swine! I've a good mind to take their basket back and chuck it at their heads! If they wanted to put their rotten clothes somewhere while they were swimming, why didn't they bring a laundry basket? Picnic baskets are for *picnics*!'

Then, all of a sudden, he paused. A faint smile flickered across his face and eventually blossomed into an evil grin. It had just occurred to him that when the bathers got tired of splashing about in the water, making idiots of themselves, and came back to shore to change, they would discover to their horror that their clothes were gone!

'Serves the blighters right!' he chuckled. He pictured their faces when they realised they would have to go home wet and parade along the street dressed in their ridiculous bathing suits, objects of laughter and finger-pointing. His heart soared. 'That'll learn 'em!' he cried, almost choking with laughter. 'They'll know what it's like to have to skulk around like me, afraid of people seeing you.' And he danced around, delighted with his own cleverness, cackling at the bathers' misfortune.

And then, all of a sudden, he stopped dead in his tracks and his mouth fell open again. An idea had just occurred to him, so marvellous that he gaped in astonishment. 'That's it!' he gasped. 'I've got their clothes!' He ran about the clearing, picking up first one piece of clothing and then another, examining each with care. Eventually, with a look of triumph, he held up a bathing robe made of brown flannel with a loose hood attached. Quickly, he slipped it on and pulled the hood over his head. 'He-he-he!' he sniggered. 'What a great idea! I am no longer Pugnax the cockroach! I am now, to all intents and purposes, Friar Pugnax! Now I can go wherever I like! It's goodbye to this infernal forest and back to the haunts of men!'

And, leaving the basket and the rest of the clothes scattered untidily around the clearing, he set off determinedly in the direction of Porzana village.

PART 2

CHAPTER 3

A STICKY ENCOUNTER

As villages go, Porzana was nothing to write home about. It had only one street, and along each side was assembled a motley collection of buildings which stared sullenly across at each other as if waiting to see whose windows would blink first. At the top end of the village the street widened slightly into what was called, more hopefully than accurately, 'the square'. Here there were a few shops – a grocer, a butcher and a baker. Just beyond these a horse-trough marked the upper limits of the village.

At the lower end, the street changed gradually into a

lane and then into a track which led away into the dark forest. Just where this change began stood The Flying Pig, the local inn which more or less defined the lower boundary of the village. This building was the largest in Porzana, built solidly of red brick and heavy timbers, with a roof of blue slate. Above the studded oak door hung a painted sign depicting a fat porker frolicking amongst the clouds, feathery wings sprouting from its shoulders. Smoke came from the chimney, showing that the inhabitants of the inn were up and about their business, and indeed, behind the shuttered windows, breakfast was in full swing.

As the village came slowly to life, a figure garbed in a brown hooded robe appeared at the edge of the forest. Pugnax had arrived.

The path he had followed through the forest was not used much and he had met with no-one along the way. Now, however, on the outskirts of the village, he paused, unsure of himself. Back in the safety of the forest the idea of stalking boldly back into civilisation had seemed a daring yet simple idea. But like many daring, simple ideas, when it came to actually implementing it, it seemed not quite so simple and just a little too daring. What if he were caught? Cockroaches were not generally treated as welcome visitors in the haunts of ordinary human beings, and the consequences of

discovery were impossible to predict. Obviously they wouldn't squash him under their shoes as they would a common run-of-the-mill cockroach – he was much too large for that – but they might easily load him down with chains and sling him into jail. Or, even worse, they might put him in a zoo to be stared at as an object of curiosity!

He shuddered at the thought, and was about to give up his plan entirely and retrace his steps when he heard, from a point a few yards behind him, a voice which said: 'Frog-face!'

Pugnax spun around and there, sitting on the stone wall at the side of the path, was a small boy with spiky hair and a dirty face, his clothes besmirched here and there with mud and grime. In his mouth was a lollipop which he manoeuvred skilfully from side to side with his tongue. Pugnax, preoccupied with his daring plan, had walked past without noticing him, but the boy had obviously got a good look at Pugnax.

'What did you say?' said Pugnax.

The boy removed the lollipop from his mouth, smearing stickiness around his already sticky chops. 'I said Frog-face!' he said, and then added after consideration: 'Although that doesn't really describe you right; you're more like one of them grasshoppers!'

Pugnax waggled his antennae angrily. 'How dare

you!' he said loudly. 'I'll have you horsewhipped, you ... you ...' Words failed him.

'And another thing,' continued the boy, pointing at Pugnax's still-quivering antennae, 'Where'd you get them eyebrows?'

Pugnax took a deep breath, turned away and began to march haughtily into the village. Glancing behind him, he noted with despair that his tormentor had hopped down from the wall and was now dogging his footsteps. Pugnax began to feel agitated. If this little blighter kept following him he would give the game away. Perhaps if he ignored him ...

CHAPTER 4

FREDDIE FENNIFEATHER

In the kitchen of The Flying Pig, Mrs Fennifeather, the landlady, sat at the breakfast table, going through the morning mail. There were several bills, a postcard from her sister, and a letter for her grown-up daughter, Aelfreda. Mrs Fennifeather looked at the letter and frowned. It was not addressed, as it should have been in her view, to 'Miss Aelfreda Fennifeather', but was instead directed simply to 'Freddie Fennifeather'. Tossing the letter across the table to her daughter who was buttering toast, she said sharply: 'Aelfreda! How many times have I told you not to give people that horrid shortened version of your name? And just look at your hair!'

Freddie combed the hair out of her eyes with her fingers. 'Oh, Mother! Don't start that again! Nobody bats an eyelid when *men* call themselves Freddie. Just because I'm a woman I'm supposed to use a name that gets stuck in the corners of people's mouths when they try to say it! I mean, what a name to be saddled with! Aelfreda Fennifeather! It sounds like the start of a tongue-twister! Something like: "Aelfreda Fennifeather fixing faucets in the foc'sle of a frigate" springs to mind.'

'Aelfreda!' cried Mrs Fennifeather, aghast. She turned to her husband who was pouring himself a cup of tea. 'Albert!' she appealed. 'Do something about your daughter!'

'Eh?' said Mr Fennifeather. 'Do something? About my daughter?'

'Albert!' cried Mrs Fennifeather. 'I've warned you about that too! Don't keep repeating everything I say!'

'Repeating?' said Mr Fennifeather, staring innocently at his wife. 'Everything you say?'

Mrs Fennifeather lapsed into silence and contented herself with opening her eyes wide and staring angrily at her husband. Mr Fennifeather, not to be outdone, opened his eyes wide and stared back.

'Oh!' shouted Mrs Fennifeather in exasperation, striking the table with her hand. 'You're the limit! Not only do you repeat everything I say, but you even repeat everything I look!'

'Everything you ...' Mr Fennifeather began, but thought better of it when his wife rose menacingly from the table with the bread-knife in her hand. She pointed to the kitchen door. 'If you've quite finished your breakfast, Albert Fennifeather, go and open the shutters and the bar door. It's past opening-time and I have to get my pies out of the oven.'

'Ah! Right!' said Mr Fennifeather, finishing his tea. 'Come on, Freddie. You can help me stock the shelves.'

'Coming,' said Freddie, getting up, still munching toast.

Father and daughter went out into the bar. Mr Fennifeather unbarred the door which opened onto the village street while Freddie opened back the window-shutters. As she did so she spied, coming along the street, a figure which she took to be a monk, closely followed by a young boy whom she recognised as Horace Catchfly.

'Little terror!' she muttered. 'Pestering people again. If I could only catch hold of him ...'

* * *

Just under the sign of The Flying Pig, the boy made a facetious remark concerning the shape of Pugnax's legs and the Prince whirled around furiously. 'Get away, you little beast!' he hissed, 'or I'll have you hung up by the heels and flayed alive!'

The boy stopped, stuck out his tongue and sang out in a jeering voice: 'Yah! You'd have to catch me first! And that's something you couldn't do! For one thing, you're too fat, and for another thing – ow! wow! ooh!'

From the doorway where the boy had stopped a slender arm had emerged, and the shapely hand on the end of it had grasped him firmly by the ear. It was this that had cut him short in his account of Pugnax's physical shortcomings. 'Ooh! lemme go!' he bawled.

From the doorway, Freddie Fennifeather appeared, still maintaining her grip on the boy's ear.

'Horace Catchfly!' she said angrily. 'How many times have I warned you about calling people names and behaving in such a disgraceful way?'

'Ow! Woo! Leggo!' cried Horace.

'I will when you apologise to this gentleman.'

'Yow! Eee! All right! I apologise! Woo! Lemme go!'

'Promise to behave yourself in future!' demanded Freddie.

'I promise! Yow! Gimme back my ear!'

Freddie released him and he immediately ran off up

the street, but once at a safe distance he stuck his thumbs in his ears and waggled his fingers derisively.

'Yah!' he shouted. 'Grasshopper! Eyebrows! And sucks to you, Miss Aelfreda Fancypants!'

'What!' cried Freddie, outraged. 'Come back here!' And with that, she took off up the street in hot pursuit of the boy, who was already disappearing into the distance.

Pugnax stared after them. He hoped sincerely that the girl would catch the little so-and-so and boil him in oil, but judging by the speed he had disappeared at, there wasn't much hope of that.

But just at that moment a new sensation came to Pugnax which banished all that had gone before. From the doorway of The Flying Pig came a scent so delicious that it brought tears to Pugnax's eyes. It was a fragrance which he had not smelled for ever such a long time. It brought back memories of cold winter evenings in front of the fire and hot dinners that made you feel like a newly-lit candle. This scent had always been one of his favourites, and now, after all he had been through, it completely overpowered him. It was freshly-baked steak-and-kidney pie. Following his nose, as if drawn by a magnet, he entered the doorway of The Flying Pig and strode purposefully to the bar.

CHAPTER 5

PIES FOR PUGNAX

Mrs Fennifeather had always been proud of her skill in the kitchen, and she was highly flattered when Mr Fennifeather came through from the bar and informed her that the customer outside had ordered another of her steak-and-kidney pies. She prided herself on those pies and it was nice to know they were appreciated. This feeling of gratification increased when the order came in for a third pie, but Mrs Fennifeather began to think it rather odd when a fourth was demanded.

'Surely no-one can eat four pies!' she exclaimed, but business was business and if a customer wanted four pies who was she to complain?

Outside in the bar, Mr Fennifeather stared at his customer with a sort of horrified fascination. Pugnax had never been very tidy in his eating habits and the table at which he now sat was covered with crumbs and bits of pastry. In addition to the three steak-and-kidney pies he had just demolished, he had also swallowed an equal number of pints of stout, and had just called for another to accompany the fourth pie he had ordered.

'I never seen anything like it!' Mr Fennifeather muttered under his breath. He placed a foaming glass in front of Pugnax and stepped back. 'Your pie will be here in a moment, sir.'

Pugnax nodded and took a noisy slurp of his stout.

'You'll forgive my asking, sir,' ventured Mr Fennifeather, 'but you're a stranger in these parts, I believe ...'

Pugnax gave a start and pulled his robe closer around himself. He waggled his antennae and peered out from the depths of his hood. 'I'm not in the habit of answering questions, my man,' he said haughtily. 'Kindly confine yourself to your duties.'

Mr Fennifeather stepped back and gave a little bow. 'I beg your pardon, sir,' he said, 'I didn't mean to pry.'

He returned to his place behind the bar. Obviously this gentleman was *somebody*. Anybody who was nobody wouldn't dare to speak to him in such insolent tones. Albert Fennifeather knew quality when he saw it!

At that moment the bar door was thrust open and Freddie came in, pink-faced and short of breath.

'Why, Freddie!' said Mr Fennifeather. 'You're worn out! What've you been up to?'

'I've been chasing that little horror Horace Catchfly. He escaped me again, of course! He was insulting this gentleman,' she said, indicating Pugnax.

'The little brat!' said Mr Fennifeather. 'I'll have to

talk to his parents and ...'

'Never mind *him*!' interrupted Freddie. 'I've just heard something much more important. It's all over the village! Prince Pugnax up at Porzana Castle has been declared officially dead!'

'WHAT?' spluttered Pugnax, jumping to his feet, spraying droplets of stout across the table.

'Yes,' went on Freddie, 'and Bembex of Bellonia is to take his place at the castle! I must go and tell Mother!'

Pugnax stared after her as she disappeared into the kitchen. For a moment he was speechless. Then, turning to Mr Fennifeather, he said, 'Who is that girl?'

'Girl?' repeated Mr Fennifeather. 'Oh! You mean Freddie! That's our barmaid – and my daughter, of course.'

'What she said just now – it can't be true!'

'Can't be true? Oh, I don't know, sir; she's not in the habit of making things up ...'

Pugnax lapsed into silence. When Freddie reappeared from the kitchen, bearing a steak-and-kidney pie, he got to his feet and tottered to the bar.

'Your pie, sir,' said Freddie with a smile, placing the plate on the counter in front of Pugnax.

'What you said a moment ago ...' began Pugnax, 'about Bembex ...'

'Oh yes,' said Freddie, 'isn't it terrible? Pugnax, with

all his faults – and he had many –'

'Now look here!' objected Pugnax.

'wasn't a despoiler of the countryside like this Bembex,' went on Freddie, taking no notice of the interruption. 'I hear that he cut down all the trees on his estate in Bellonia and sold them to a paper mill. Imagine! Turning beautiful trees into newspapers and trashy novels!'

Pugnax sank onto a bar-stool and stared forlornly at his pie. 'But they can't say a fellow's dead just because he hasn't been around for a while,' he said weakly. 'Can they?'

Freddie shrugged. She picked up a glass and began to polish it. 'It appears they can. That's the law. It does seem hard, though. Poor old Pugnax! He might have been fat and lazy and greedy and mean, and more besides, but when all is said and done ...' She stopped in mid-sentence. Pugnax had got to his feet again and seemed to be choking.

'Is something the matter, sir?' asked Mr Fennifeather from the end of the bar. 'Piece of pie gone down the wrong way?'

Pugnax made no answer. From under the shadow of his hood, he stared out at Freddie. 'How dare you?' he choked.

'How dare I what?' said Freddie.

'How dare you speak about your betters in that fashion?

Such insults! And from a common barmaid!'

Mr Fennifeather drew in his breath sharply. He knew his daughter well and though she was an easygoing girl as a rule she had a terrible temper, and the sort of remark just made by this customer was exactly the thing to spark it off.

Freddies eyes flashed as she drew herself up to her full five-foot-three. Mr Fennifeather winced. When Freddie drew herself up like that, strong men ran for cover and even the cat walked carefully.

'What do you mean by "betters"?' she demanded, in cold, measured tones. 'And "common barmaid"?'

Pugnax was sharp enough to recognise barely suppressed fury when he saw it, and in the face of it his outrage evaporated. Ordinarily, persons he considered his social inferiors held no terror for him, but in this case, he reasoned, it might be better to err on the side of caution. He had better try to mollify this wench; he didn't like the way those sparks were coming from her eyes.

'Er ... that is ...' he said, with a little forced laugh, 'I actually meant to say –'

'Just what's wrong with being a barmaid?' persisted Freddie menacingly.

It dawned upon Pugnax that he had put his foot in it. 'Oh! Nothing!' he blustered. 'Nothing at all! A very worthwhile occupation! Actually, I know a lot of people who ought to be barmaids. I was, once engaged to a princess who would have been much better off as a barmaid. In fact,' he added coaxingly, 'you and she could quite easily change places and no-one would know the difference!' And he sniggered at the idea.

Mr Fennifeather decided it was time to intervene before things got out of hand. 'Now, now, Freddie,' he said soothingly, 'you mustn't pick the customers up on every little thing they say. The gentleman didn't mean anything, and he's been generous enough to say that you could quite easily be a princess–'

Freddie turned on her father. 'I don't want to be a princess,' she said coldly. 'I'm quite happy as I am.'

At that moment, Mrs Fennifeather appeared at the kitchen door, a fish-slice in her hand. 'Is anything wrong?' she asked. 'I thought I heard voices raised ...'

'Nothing, my dear, nothing,' said Mr Fennifeather, ushering his wife back into the kitchen. 'A slight misunderstanding, that's all!'Once inside the kitchen, Mr Fennifeather pushed shut the door.

'What's going on?' demanded his wife.

'Shh! I just heard that gentleman say that he was once engaged to a princess.'

Mrs Fennifeather gasped. 'Albert! Are you sure?'

'I am. The fact is, I've been watching him. I knew

there was something about him – I always have had a nose for picking out the quality. Did you notice his eyebrows? A sure sign of breeding!'

'What nonsense!' Mrs Fennifeather objected. 'Why, old Jacob Stobbins up at the castle has eyebrows like scrubbing-brushes and no more breeding than a turnip!'

'Well, you just take it from me,' said Mr Fennifeather. 'This fellow's different. You can tell by the insolent way he has about him that he's someone – a lord or a duke at least – and, what's more,' he added confidingly, 'I believe he's taken a shine to our Freddie!'

'Aelfreda?' cried Mrs Fennifeather. 'I don't believe it! No-one would take a shine to Aelfreda, let alone a duke or whatever you say he is. She's not ladylike enough.'

Mr Fennifeather gave a long wink. 'Ladylike or not, you just wait! He as good as told her that she'd make a pretty fair princess!'

'Princess!' squawked Mrs Fennifeather. 'I believe you've gone simple in the brain!' She moved stealthily to the door, opened it a crack and peeped out.

'Hmm,' she said. 'I don't know about breeding, but he's certainly a fair hand at feeding! Look at the way he's guzzling that steak-and-kidney pie. You'd swear he hadn't eaten a bite for years! And why's he got that hood over his head?'

Mr Fennifeather laid a finger alongside his nose.

'All the quality travel that way,' he said knowingly. '*Incognito* they call it.'

'Well,' said Mrs Fennifeather, 'I don't know about that, but I do know that he's eaten enough pies for four ordinary men. And what about all that stout he's drunk? Have you seen the colour of his money yet?'

Mr Fennifeather considered. 'Perhaps you're right, my dear. After all, business is business. I suppose it won't hurt to drop a hint.'

*   *   *

Freddie was busy stacking bottles of lemonade on a shelf as Mr Fennifeather came back into the bar, whistling softly to himself. The storm seemed to have subsided and peace reigned once more. Pugnax's shock at finding himself declared dead had also passed, and, realising that there was nothing he could do about it, he had put the matter aside for the moment and was concentrating on his fourth pie. He glanced up as Mr Fennifeather came in. 'Ah! just draw me another pint of stout, my good man,' he said affably.

'Straightaway, sir,' answered Mr Fennifeather. 'But before I do, there's one small thing I might mention. It's by way of being a rule of the house, so to speak, that customers settle their bills after three pints. And seeing as you've had four already, not to mention four pies, I think it might be as well to square things up.'

'Oh, don't worry about that!' said Pugnax airily. 'We'll settle that later!'

Mr Fennifeather began to smell a rat. He had had plenty of experience of customers whose pockets turned out to be not so well-lined as their owners had suggested. 'I think,' he said stonily, 'that we'll settle up now, sir, if it's all the same to you.'

Pugnax shifted uneasily on his stool. He was not quite sure what to do. It went against the grain with him to settle bills of any kind, and present conditions were such that he could not settle this bill even if he wanted to. He had no money and no possible way of getting any. The only thing to do was to brazen it out.

'Now look here, my man ...' he began, in his most aristocratic voice.

The colour rose in Mr Fennifeather's cheeks. He was quite happy to be "my-manned" by a paying customer, but things were beginning to look different now.

'We'll have a bit less of the "my man", if you don't mind,' he growled. 'What I want to know is have you got money to pay for what you ate and drank?'

'Of course I've got money!' said Pugnax petulantly. 'It's just that ... well ... er... the fact is ... I've left it at home!'

'I see,' said Mr Fennifeather, nodding his head. 'And

just where might "home" be?'

'My home,' said Pugnax proudly, 'is Porzana Castle.'

'Oh, yes? And I suppose the next thing you'll tell us is you're Prince Pugnax of the same address, eh? Ho! Ho! That'll give us a good laugh, won't it? Especially since we've just heard you're dead!'

'Now look here!' protested Pugnax.

'No, you look here!' countered Mr Fennifeather. 'I've met your sort before. You go around pretending to be someone you're not; you worm your way into public houses where you eat steak-and-kidney pies and drink pints of stout, and then you sneak off without paying! That's your game isn't it? I took you at first to be a gentleman, but I see now that you're nothing more than a ragamuffin vagabond! In short, a common tramp!'

'Tramp?' spluttered Pugnax, outraged, sending particles of pie whistling across the bar. 'I'll have you know that I am none other than the noble Pugnax, Prince of Porzana, revered and respected by all who know me! I've never been so insulted in all my life! Well, I have,' he added as an afterthought, 'but not by anyone of such low social standing as a barbarian barkeeper!'

Freddie rose up from behind the bar where she had just finished stacking the lemonade. 'Don't you dare speak about my father in those terms!' she snapped. 'He's an honest man – which it seems you are not!'

'Take it easy, Freddie,' said Mr Fennifeather. 'I can fight my own battles, which is what I intend to start doing right now!' And with that, he began to roll up his sleeves. 'Barbarian, am I?' he growled. 'Barkeeper, am I?'

Mr Fennifeather's arms were like thick ropes with knots in them. Pugnax gulped as he looked at them. He waggled his antennae nervously. 'Now, now,' he said in a wheedling tone. 'There's no need to get excited ...' And with that, deciding that a good run would be better than a bad stand, he hopped down off his stool and darted for the nearest door, which happened to be the one opening into the kitchen.

'Stop!' roared Mr Fennifeather.

'Come back!' cried Freddie.

Pugnax paid no heed. He thrust open the door, blundered through, and suddenly found himself clasped in a strong pair of arms – those of Mrs Fennifeather!

'OOF!' gasped the landlady, staring at her unlooked-for prisoner. 'What's all this?'

'Lemme go!' cried Pugnax, struggling to make his escape.

But Mrs Fennifeather, though taken unawares, was alert enough to realise that the object which had just thrust itself into her embrace was none other than the pie-eater whom she and her husband had been discussing. With great presence of mind, she decided that the best thing to do was to hang on to him. So, as he spun around in order to free himself, she grasped him by the cloak which still concealed him from the world's gaze. Pugnax made a great effort and tore himself free, but found to his horror that his cloak did not come with him.

At that moment, the kitchen door swung open once more and Mr Fennifeather burst in.

Pugnax was trapped. A Fennifeather before him, a Fennifeather behind him, and nowhere to go! And, what was worse, without his cloak and hood, he was revealed in his true form!

Mr Fennifeather gaped.

Freddie, shoving in behind him, goggled.

Mrs Fennifeather groaned.

'A *cockroach*!' they cried in unison.

PART 3

CHAPTER 6

A CALLER FOR MCCRACKEN

Deep in the forest, in a clearing surrounded by dense growths of beech and sycamore, sat the snug little cottage of Lucifer John McCracken. The grass and weeds grew thick and lush here – the rabbits and deer were afraid to come too near the wizard's home, and Lucifer John himself never dreamed of cutting what he regarded as his 'flower garden'. From the encroaching forest, brambles sent out long snaky stems into the clearing. Some had rooted amongst the grass and were busy sending up new shoots, glistening and purple in their spiny youth.

All was silent around the little cottage. High overhead a kestrel hovered, his sharp black eyes on the alert for a careless mouse or vole. An orange-tip butterfly fluttered lazily across the clearing, and under the shade of the trees flies droned sleepily. But apart from these signs of life, nothing disturbed the tranquility of the little glade. Although the sun was high in the sky, there was as yet no smoke in Lucifer John's chimney, for the wizard had not yet got up.

Suddenly, with a flash of black and white feathers, a magpie swooped into the clearing. Chattering noisily, he perched on a low branch of the great oak which overhung the cottage, and flicked his tail up and down jauntily. He cocked his head to one side, rolled his eye from side to side and then, leaving his perch, fluttered down to the ground. With a swagger, he stalked up to Lucifer John's door.

A rat had eaten a hole in the bottom of the door some time ago and the wizard had never got around to repairing it, so the magpie was able to enter the cottage. Once inside, he peered around in the gloom. Lucifer John had little in the way of furniture. In the centre of the room stood a simple table made from rough boards and upon this lay a crust of bread and a rind of cheese, the remnants of a frugal supper. At each side of the wide fireplace was an upside-down butter-box serving as a chair, and against the far wall lay a large black oaken chest. In an alcove at one side of the room, Lucifer John had his bed, and he lay in it now, hidden beneath the bed-clothes.

The magpie clicked his tongue disapprovingly. Up all night star-gazing or some other such nonsense, I'll be bound! he thought grimly.

With a flick of his tail, he hopped up onto the end of the bed and let out a loud and prolonged chatter. There was a faint stirring under the blankets and then, slowly, a bony white hand appeared, followed by a tangle of white hair and, finally, an indignant face. A bleary eye fastened on the magpie, who was now preening his feathers unconcernedly.

'Bird,' said the old man in a pained voice, 'if I had ever felt the need for an alarm clock, I would have purchased one of the excellent models which are available in all the neighbouring villages. However, since I have never wanted such an object, how is it that you take it upon yourself to fill that role in my life? Or, in other words, *what the devil do you mean by waking me up*?'

'You should have been up long ago,' the magpie chuckled. 'The only people entitled to be in bed at this hour are badgers, bats and burglars, all of whom have to make their livings by night. Anyway, the reason I woke you is that you have a visitor.'

'I know,' growled the wizard. 'You!'

The magpie gave another chuckle. 'I don't mean me. There's another one on the way. I thought I'd better come and warn you.'

Lucifer John sat out on the edge of his bed and scratched his head. 'What kind of visitor?'

'Oh! Didn't I make that clear? A human.'

'I gathered that much. Can't you be a bit more precise?'

The magpie considered. 'Hmm ... let me see. I believe she's a hen, that is – I beg your pardon – a female. Other than that, well, you know how it is, all you humans look pretty much the same to me.'

Lucifer John blew out his breath. 'You know, if I wanted visitors, I would live in a town. One of the reasons I live here in the forest is to keep as far away as possible from visitors!'

At that moment, a knock came to the door and the wizard stood up. 'I suppose I'll have to see who she is.'

'Don't you think you'd better put some trousers on first?' said the magpie. 'Or do you plan to greet her in your night attire?'

'I don't plan to greet her at all!' grumbled Lucifer John. 'But I suppose you're right. The proprieties must be observed. Just a minute!' he added with a shout, as another knock sounded at the door.

'She seems rather impatient,' remarked the magpie, as Lucifer John unlatched the door and peered out at the unexpected form of Aelfreda Fennifeather.

'Good afternoon,' said Freddie. 'Are you the wizard McCracken?'

Lucifer John stared at her from under his eyebrows. 'I am Lucifer John McCracken,' he said proudly. 'Bone-setter, charm-maker, herb-gatherer, star-gazer and caster of spells. I can also, amongst other things, converse with the birds of the air, prophesy the weather, play the flute and deliver babies! And lately,' he added, 'I have learned to dance the Sailor's Hornpipe!'

'Oh!' said Freddie, with a half-smile.

Lucifer John glared. 'I know what that "Oh!" means. You think I'm bragging! Would you prefer if I told you I was an ordinary man? That would be untrue. Does a lion prowl around in the jungle saying "Miaouw!" and pretending to be a pussycat? Of course not! He roars because he's a lion and proud of it! And doesn't care who knows it! Well,' he finished gruffly, 'it's the same with me.'

'I'm sorry,' said Freddie, suitably chastened. 'I didn't mean to ... um ...' She decided to change the subject. 'My name,' she said brightly, 'is Freddie Fennifeather.'

'Freddie?' repeated the wizard. 'Funny name for a girl. That's a boy's name.'

'No, it's not!' said Freddie sharply. 'It's a name for anyone who wants to use it. And I'm not a girl, I'm a woman.'

This time it was Lucifer John who smiled. 'I beg your pardon,' he said. 'I didn't mean to insult you. I tend to think of everybody younger than myself as boys and girls.'

'Well, I'm sorry too,' said Freddie. 'I didn't mean to snap; I have an awful temper.'

'Oh, don't mention it,' said the wizard. 'I like to see a bit of spirit in young people. Come in, come in,' he added, opening the door wide and standing to one side. As Freddie stepped in, the magpie flew out, brushing her with his wing as he passed. 'Confounded bird!' cried Lucifer John. 'Absolutely no manners!'

Once inside, the wizard indicated a butter-box beside the fire and invited his visitor to sit down. 'Would you like some breakfast?' he asked.

'No, thank you,' returned Freddie. 'But I could manage some lunch.'

'Hmm ... well, I'll give you some breakfast and you can pretend it's lunch! If you'll get the fire started, I'll slip down to the stream and check my fish-lines.' And, muttering to himself, the wizard disappeared out the door.

Freddie cleared away the ashes, drew some sticks

from a bundle which lay beside the fireplace, and soon had a merry blaze crackling in the grate. She gazed around the room. It didn't seem much like a wizard's house – at least not what she imagined a wizard's house *should* look like; somehow she thought it ought to look more mysterious, with books, and glass jars, and bunches of herbs and so on, and perhaps a tame raven croaking on the table. But this just looked like the abode of a poor old man. As she was thinking these thoughts, Lucifer John reappeared, carrying in each hand a fine speckled trout.

'Do you like fish?' he enquired.

'Yes,' said Freddie.

'I prefer eels myself,' said the wizard. 'Much tastier. But one can't be too choosy.' He balanced an iron frying-pan over the fire and, after cleaning the fish, he placed them side by side in it.

'I knew an Oswald Fennifeather once,' he said absently, as the fish began to sizzle. 'Any relation?'

'Yes,' said Freddie, 'he was my grandfather.'

'I remember him,' said the wizard. 'He came to me years ago, complaining of a toothache, only he couldn't be sure which tooth it was. But that didn't matter; I soon cured him.'

'How?' asked Freddie, interested.

'I started at one side of his jaw with a pair of pliers and

began pulling teeth until I got the right one. By that time, as it happened, there were only two or three left, so I pulled them out too, to spare him any further trouble. He said afterwards that it was the most complete cure for toothache he'd ever come across.'

Before long the fish were done, and, with the tip of his knife, the old man flicked them out of the pan onto the plates which Freddie held out.

'Now, young lady,' he began as he pulled the backbone out of his trout, 'what can I do for you?'

'It's about Pugnax,' said Freddie, licking her fingers.

Lucifer John cocked an enquiring eyebrow. 'What do you know about Pugnax?'

'Well, I know that you turned him into a cockroach and –'

'One moment!' the wizard interrupted, holding up his hand. 'You are mistaken. Pugnax turned himself into a cockroach – all by himself. I had very little to do with it.'

'He blames you.'

The wizard sighed. 'That doesn't surprise me at all.'

'Well,' continued Freddie, 'couldn't you just change him back into a human being? It's very important.'

The wizard regarded Freddie askance. 'Pugnax of Porzana was *never* a human being, except in a very loose sense of the term. And as for changing him into one, it's not as easy as you think. You can't simply snap your fingers and transform cockroaches into people. And anyway, why this sudden interest in the former Prince of Porzana?'

'He's staying in our house at the moment,' explained Freddie. 'The poor creature is terribly unhappy.'

'Well? Just boot him out. That's what he deserves.'

'Oh! We couldn't! Besides, we need him.'

'Need him?' repeated Lucifer John, his mouth full of fish. 'What d'you need *him* for?'

'Haven't you heard? Porzana Castle has been taken over by Bembex, Pugnax's nephew.'

'Bembex? Isn't he the fellow who cut down all the trees in Bellonia and sold them to a paper mill?'

Freddie nodded. 'The very one. And now he intends to do the same in Porzana. Porzana Forest, to be exact.'

Lucifer John dropped his knife. 'Do the same in Porzana?' he gasped. 'Porzana Forest?'

'Please don't repeat everything I say,' said Freddie. 'You sound like my father.'

Lucifer John got to his feet and paced restlessly around the room. Suddenly, he stopped and said: 'What's all this got to do with Pugnax?'

'Pugnax has promised that if he's changed back into human form and reinstated in Porzana he'll turn the forest into a nature reserve.'

The ghost of a smile played across Lucifer John's

face. 'And you believe him?'

Freddie blushed; it isn't nice to have someone suggest that you are perhaps more gullible than you ought to be. 'Well,' she said defensively, 'at least he's saying it! That's better than what Bembex is saying!'

Lucifer John sat down again and began picking at the remains of his fish.

'Well?' said Freddie, after a pause. 'What do you say?'

The wizard looked up, but made no answer. He was obviously thinking deeply. After a while, he put his plate on the floor, got up and walked across to the great oak chest in the corner of the room. Lifting the latch, he threw back the lid and extracted a large, dusty, leather-bound book. He blew the dust off it, opened it, flicked through several pages and, finding the place he wanted, read carefully for several moments, pausing now and then to look at the ceiling, scratch his head or mutter to himself. Then, closing the book, he replaced it, shut down the lid of the chest, fastened the latch and returned to his butter-box. Freddie looked at him expectantly.

The wizard picked up a stick and began to poke the fire. 'There *is* a spell I could use,' he said slowly, 'but it requires a number of charms – three to be exact. Two of them – a wild-cat's claw and a spider's skin – I can get myself, but the third might prove difficult.'

'What is it?' asked Freddie.

'The shell of a hatched eagle's egg.'

'The shell of a hatched eagle's egg?' repeated Freddie, realising that *she* was now beginning to sound like her father. 'Where do we get one of those?'

Lucifer John shrugged. 'Eagles used to be fairly plentiful around here in the old days, but I haven't seen one now for quite some time.'

'But surely there must be a nest somewhere,' said Freddie. 'There just has to be!'

'I believe there is one – in Porzana Forest, strangely enough. However, I'm too busy to go gallivanting off after eagles' eggs just now, so I'm afraid it's up to you.'

'Me? But how would I find it?' said Freddie. 'I wouldn't even know where to start!'

'There is just one chance ...' said the wizard, scratching his head and looking doubtful.

'Yes?' said Freddie eagerly.

'Black Donald.'

'Black Don–?'

'Black Donald,' said Lucifer John decisively.

'Who is Black Donald?'

'Ah!' said Lucifer John with a sigh. 'That's a good question. Another good one would be: "Who is Lucifer John McCracken?" And if you want a really tough one, ask yourself: "Who is Aelfreda Fennifeather?"'

Freddie furrowed her brow. 'I'm afraid I don't understand.'

Lucifer John smiled. 'I wish people would admit that fact more often,' he murmured. 'Nowadays, people seem to understand everything, or claim to, anyway. I've been around for a long time and I don't think I understand very much at all! And I don't think I really want to! I know, for example, that since I learned to understand the language of the birds, their songs don't sound so sweet, and ... well, never mind. As for your question: Black Donald is ... well, he's Black Donald, and if anyone can get the shell of an eagle's egg, it's him. He lives somewhere in the Black Coomb – nobody knows exactly where.'

'Well?' demanded Freddie, 'can't *you* ask him to get it?'

Lucifer John coughed and scratched his head. 'Unfortunately, Black Donald and myself are not on speaking terms – we had a slight misunderstanding some time back over some wild mushrooms.'

'How childish!' said Freddie.

Lucifer John drew himself up. 'I'll thank you to keep your opinions to yourself, young lady,' he said stiffly.

Freddie winced. The last thing she wanted to do was antagonise the wizard. 'I'm sorry,' she said. 'It's none of my business.'

Lucifer John seemed mollified. 'If you want the egg-shell, you'll have to go and see him yourself,' he said, then added, 'and I warn you, he's a strange character.'

Freddie stood up. 'Well, there's no time like the present. How will I find him?'

'That's hard to say. If he doesn't want to be found, you – or anybody else – won't find him. All you can do is go into the Black Coomb. He'll know you're there and he might decide to talk to you. Then again,' he concluded, 'he might not.'

Freddie looked doubtful. 'That doesn't sound very hopeful.'

Lucifer John shrugged. 'There's no other way. You must only hope for the best.'

After listening carefully to the wizard's directions, Freddie took her leave.

Leaning in the doorway, Lucifer John watched her as she strode off determinedly into the forest. 'She's quite something,' he said, cupping his chin in his hand. 'Black Donald had better look to himself! Who knows? Something good may yet come through Pugnax.' He considered for a while. 'Perhaps I should pay old Pugnax a visit. He may have a role to play in all this ...'

CHAPTER 7

A STORM IN THE COOMB

As Freddie took leave of Lucifer John, she was in high spirits. The sun was shining, there was a gentle breeze blowing, and it was nice to be out of the village, wandering around in the countryside, following the course of the little river which, the wizard had told her, would lead her into the Black Coomb. A river is always a pleasant and interesting companion to walk beside, and this one chuckled merrily, delighted to have Freddie for company in its watery meanderings. Rushes and sweet flags fringed its banks, and dragonflies darted to and fro, flying jewels of azure and emerald. Here and there, where the stream widened into limpid pools, pond-skaters glided across the surface, and in the amber depths, dark trout-shadows dashed under cover of the bank at Freddie's approach. Everything was a delight to the eye, and the bubbling songs of reed-warblers and willow-wrens completed the idyllic scene.

Coupled with all this, Freddie had the satisfaction of knowing that she was doing something worthwhile and important, and underlying everything else was that wonderful, half-nervous, half-exciting feeling which we call adventure. All in all, she felt so exuberant that when a kingfisher flashed along the surface of the river like a bolt of blue light, she laughed out loud.

'How marvellous to have a mission!' she said to herself. 'If I can just find this Black Donald and get him to show me where the eagle's nest is, I can save Porzana Forest and get Pugnax changed back into a person. Poor Pugnax!' she sighed. 'How he must have suffered! I wonder if Lucifer John was right about his being untrustworthy ...'

With thoughts such as these, she whiled away the time as she walked. Gradually, the little river became narrower and the forest began to close in on either side. Until now, the going had been easy and pleasant, but now it was getting a little harder. Brambles and briars caught at her clothes and the undergrowth became so dense that at times she was forced to wade into the water in order to make progress.

When the sun began to sink in the west, she had been walking for quite some time and she was beginning to think she should be nearing her destination. She arrived at a spot where the river was almost completely blocked by two huge boulders. Only in mid-stream was the flow of water unrestricted and there it ran fast and deep. Freddie paused. She recognised this place because

Lucifer John had described it to her: it marked the entrance to the Black Coomb. What lay ahead seemed strange and forbidding, and for the first time she began to ask herself what she was doing here. The truth is, it was beginning to get dark and the breeze had turned cold, and she was thinking how nice it would be to be at home in the kitchen of The Flying Pig, sitting by the fire, drinking cocoa. But, shaking off these feelings, she took a deep breath, put her best foot forward, and, skirting around one of the boulders, stepped forward into the Black Coomb.

The trees grew thicker here, and their foliage was more luxuriant, but a narrow path, springing out from the water's edge, made the passage easier. Two birds – she thought they looked like pigeons – flew up in front of her and, with a great clattering of wings, soared away over the tree-tops.

* * *

At the top of the craggy slope which formed the eastern side of the Coomb, a man sat on his heels, staring intently at the scene below him. His black clothing matched the colour of his hair, and his two black eyes glittered in a face bronzed by wind and sun.

It was the noisy clattering of the two woodpigeons which had first alerted him to an intrusion into his domain. Something – or someone – moving through the trees had obviously disturbed the birds and, since then, other signs had marked the intruder's passage: a jay had screeched, a magpie had chattered, and now a blackbird's clarion call rang out shrilly through the greenery.

The man crouched forward, taking his weight on one knee, a frown across his face. At his side a black dog, standing silent till now, gave a barely audible whimper, pricked up his ears and curled his tail into the shape of a question-mark, which was his way of saying: What?

The man placed a hand gently on the dog's head, and spoke in a low, quiet voice: 'Steady, Pharaoh; someone comes.'

The dog straightened his tail and then formed the question-mark again. This time he meant: Who?

The man shook his head. 'I don't know. We'll wait. It'll be dark soon ...'

*   *   *

As the sun sank low in the west, a great darkness appeared in the north. Huge rolling clouds of grey and black spread quickly across the sky and a strange heaviness filled the air. It seemed almost as if the darkening heavens were sinking upon the earth, stifling all beneath them.

Freddie began to feel a little weak, and a fine film of sweat broke out across her face. 'Just my luck!' she said to herself. 'A storm coming.'

Suddenly, without warning, a blinding flash lit up the world around her, protesting against the gathering gloom. Then, a split second later, a great thud fell upon the forest, as if a giant fist had hammered on the roof of the sky. Freddie staggered and fell to one knee, her heart pounding, her hands raised above her head as though to ward off the thunderclap. Birds who had taken up their night-time roosts in the trees and under-growth abandoned their shelters and flew madly away into the gloom, not knowing where they went. Some-where in the distance, a cock pheasant crowed loudly: 'Cock-cock-cock!' as he fled terror-stricken through the forest.

Freddie got to her feet, breathing heavily. 'Good God Almighty!' she gasped. 'That frightened the life out of me!'

So far, no rain had fallen, but now, great drops began to splash down, bouncing from leaves and twigs on to the forest floor. But these were merely scouts, path-finders for the great army of drops which followed a moment later in a steady, drenching deluge.

Freddie looked around, water streaming from her hair and running down her neck. It was almost dark now, and she would have to move fast if she was to find shelter. But where? Her eye fell on a large oak growing nearby, its ancient trunk gnarled and twisted. Its leafy canopy was wide and spreading and, although not completely waterproof, it seemed to be throwing off the worst of the downpour.

'Any port in a storm, as they say,' she said, making up her mind. And, picking her way through the bluebells and dog's mercury which carpeted the ground, she made her way to the tree.

But as she approached it, a blinding silver light flashed before her eyes, a terrifying blast cracked through the air, and the sickening smell of sulphur filled her nose and mouth. She glanced up in time to see a black shape hurtling towards her, felt a great blow across her body, and then – no more.

PART 4

CHAPTER 8

BEMBEX IN BUSINESS

Bembex, Baron of Bellonia, having arrived at Porzana Castle, found his newly-acquired home empty. The rooms were damp and cold and the beds musty, but the Baron was undaunted. On his way to the castle, he had passed through Porzana Forest, and had noted with satisfaction that it contained much oak, beech and chestnut – all trees which could be converted into valuable timber. Even when the faithful Parker, who had accompanied his master from Bellonia, announced that supper would consist of nothing more than mashed potatoes, Bembex refused to be dispirited.

'Never mind, Parker,' he said cheerfully. 'It won't be long until we're dining on the fat of the land. Just wait till the trees begin to fall and the money starts to roll in! And speaking of that,' he added, 'send for that gardener – Hobbins or Stobbins or whatever his name is. The sooner he gets to work, the better!'

*   *   *

Jacob Stobbins was not a talkative man. He made it a general rule never to use two words where one would do, and, indeed, never to use even the one whenever a nod or a grunt would suffice.

Having explained what he wanted done, Bembex regarded him quizzically. 'Well? You've got your instructions. Haven't you anything to say?'

Mr Stobbins shrugged.

'You do know how to speak, I take it?' pursued the Baron.

Mr Stobbins nodded.

'I mean,' said Bembex acidly, 'you're not *dumb*, are you?'

Mr Stobbins shook his head.

Bembex glared. 'Well, then! You have your orders. Get on with it!'

Mr Stobbins stayed where he was. He seemed to be turning something over in his mind. At last, obviously deciding that there was no way of imparting his point of view other than by speaking, he said: 'Lot of trees.'

'Yes, there are a lot of trees,' said Bembex. 'And when you've cut 'em, there'll be a lot of timber, and that means a lot of money. So let's get started!'

Mr Stobbins took a deep breath. The Baron had obviously failed to grasp the point. His lips moved silently, as if he were trying to decide on the shortest way of putting his next speech. At last, he muttered: 'One axe.'

'One axe?' repeated Bembex. 'What's that supposed to mean? Can't you get a saw or something?'

Mr Stobbins considered. Obviously he would have to spell things out. 'Lot of trees for one man to cut,' he explained, swaying slightly with the exertion of such a long sentence.

'Are you trying to tell me,' enquired Bembex, 'that you can't do the job?' He stared balefully at the gardener. 'Do you know what, Hobbins?' he said slowly, gritting his teeth, 'or Stobbins, or whatever your name is, I've just about had enough of you gardeners! The last one I had scoffed all my sardines, and now you're kicking up because I ask you to cut down a few trees! I mean, what exactly is the point of gardeners? Answer me that!'

Mr Stobbins gave a non-committal grunt.

'All right!' shouted Bembex. 'If it's too much for you, get some help! But get those trees cut! I want that forest turned into planks and boards in double-quick time!'

CHAPTER 9

BLACK DONALD

Very slowly, Freddie opened first one eye, then the other, and stared around her in bewilderment. She seemed to be in some kind of a bed, though a far coarser and harder one than she was used to. There was a window by her side, and she could see that it was dark outside. In the room, however, a merry fire crackled, throwing a soft, cosy light around. Near the fire was a black shape and, when Freddie moved, it stirred, slowly stood up, stretched and whimpered.

Why, it's a dog! thought Freddie, and then said aloud: 'Where in the world am I?'

'Safe,' said a quiet voice from the shadow of the chimney-corner.

Freddie struggled upright in the bed to get a look at the speaker, but a piercing pain in her shoulder forced her flat again. 'What happened to me?' she asked, biting her lip.

'We found you in the forest,' said the voice. 'You were pinned under a branch – the lightning, I expect. There's nothing broken, but you'll have to take it easy for a few days.'

'I see,' said Freddie. 'Who are you?'

'It is I who must ask that question,' returned the voice. 'And what are you doing in the Black Coomb?'

Freddie was too weak to argue. 'My name is Freddie Fennifeather,' she said. 'I'm looking for someone.'

'Are you hungry?' asked the voice.

'Yes. And thirsty.'

From the shadows, a long, lean figure unfolded itself, crossed to a small cabinet and took out a plate and a mug. He placed these on a table, filled the mug from a flagon, and, from a small loaf, cut a hunk of bread which he placed on the plate.

He paused, looking at Freddie. 'Do you think you can sit up?'

'I'll try.' Gingerly, she pulled herself up in the bed and eventually got to a sitting position. She stared at the sleeves of the shirt she was wearing. 'Where did this come from? Where are my clothes?'

The figure indicated a row of garments steaming by the fire. 'I had to take them off – they were soaking. Don't worry! It was dark, and Pharaoh was here all the time,' he added, indicating the dog, who gave a short bark in agreement.

Freddie blushed, glad of the dim light. 'I wasn't worried,' she said, accepting the plate and mug. She took a mouthful of bread and sipped from the mug. It contained a sweet, fiery liquid.

'It's mead,' explained her host, noticing her puzzled expression. 'Drink it. It'll do you good.'

Freddie regarded him critically. The dark clothes he wore accentuated his wiry figure; his hair was black – or seemed so in the firelight – and his features, what she could make out of them, were dark and hooked. It was impossible to guess his age: more than twenty, she guessed, but it was hard to tell. 'Are you, by any chance, Black Donald?' she ventured.

The figure had slipped back into the shadows. 'I have been called that,' he replied, after a pause. 'Why were you seeking me?'

Freddie took another sip of mead. 'We need your help,' she answered.

'We?'

Freddie considered. 'Can't you come out here where I can see you? It's not easy talking to a shadow.'

Black Donald stood up, walked silently into the light and sat down on the floor, with his back to the fireplace. The dog came across to him, wagging his tail, and laid his head in his lap. 'Is this better?' he asked.

'Much,' said Freddie.

'Now,' said Black Donald, 'you were saying?'

Freddie, taking a bite of bread, leant back against the bedhead. 'It's a long story,' she began.

Black Donald said nothing as she told her story, but

his dark complexion turned a little paler.

'Do you mean to say,' he said finally, 'that that giant cockroach that's been wandering around in the forest all these past months is really Pugnax of Porzana?'

'You've seen him?'

Donald nodded. 'Several times. If you walk the forest as much as I do he's hard to miss – he's always sighing and groaning.'

'Well,' said Freddie, 'there you are! We have to help him!'

After a short silence, Donald said: 'Pharaoh wants to know why.'

'*Pharaoh* wants to know ...?' repeated Freddie. 'I'm afraid I don't ...'

'Look at his tail,' explained Donald.

Freddie looked. 'Why, it's a question-mark!' she exclaimed. 'I didn't know dogs could talk!'

At that, Pharaoh stretched his tail straight up in the air.

'What does that mean?' asked Freddie.

'I'd rather not say,' said Donald.

'Well anyway,' continued Freddie, 'as I was saying, we have to help Pugnax because he's promised to protect the forest if he's reinstated.'

'How can he be reinstated if he's a cockroach? I know there isn't a great deal of difference between a cockroach and the average prince, but there is *some* difference! I can't see anyone accepting a fellow with six legs and two great antennae growing out of his head as the rightful owner of Porzana Castle!'

'That's where we come in!' said Freddie, warming to the subject. 'Lucifer John has agreed to reverse the spell. We just have to find a charm for him: the shell of a hatched eagle's egg, to be precise.'

Black Donald grew silent. At length, he said quietly: 'So, it was McCracken put you up to this!'

Freddie nodded, 'Yes, why?'

'McCracken and I do not see eye to eye ...' said Donald grimly.

'Don't you think,' asked Freddie, 'that you could put your differences aside – temporarily, at least – for the sake of the forest?'

'Oh, I'd be quite willing to make friends with him,' said Donald generously, 'although it was he who started it – after all, they weren't his mushrooms! But he's an odd character, McCracken, very odd ...'

Freddie smiled. 'Well, forget about it for now. What about the eagle's egg?'

'Well,' said Donald slowly, 'as it happens – and I expect McCracken knew it when he sent you – there *is* a pair of eagles in this neck of the woods. They have their eyrie in a huge pine-tree, just where the Black Coomb runs into Porzana Forest, but their egg won't have hatched yet – and, of course, it's out of the question to try for the shell until then.'

'Of course,' Freddie agreed. 'We'll just have to wait.'

'That's all right,' said Donald, 'but if ...'

'If what?'

'I was just thinking ... if Bembex starts cutting trees anywhere near the eyrie, they may desert ...'

Freddie sat bolt upright in the bed, gasping as pain racked her shoulder. 'He must be stopped!' she cried passionately. 'He mustn't be allowed to cut the trees! Near the eyrie or anywhere else!'

'Calm down,' said Black Donald. 'I'm on your side, but it won't help to get excited. I'll take a look in the morning and see what's happening.'

With that, he got up, opened the door and, followed by Pharaoh, went out. After a few moments he reappeared, carrying an armful of logs, which he proceeded to heap onto the fire. 'These should see you through most of the night,' he said. 'Sometimes it gets cold.'

'Where are you going?' enquired Freddie.

'Don't worry about me; I often walk the Coomb at night – I don't sleep much. There's nothing to fear here, but I'll leave Pharaoh with you for company. Try and get some sleep.' And with that, he slipped silently out into the night.

PART 5

CHAPTER 10

AN EXPENSIVE EGG

Bembex stared sourly at the youth who had interrupted his breakfast (if that word could be applied to the cold mashed potatoes, a remnant of last night's supper, which Parker had served him for his morning meal).

'Well?' he said, his mouth full. 'Who are you?'

'M-m-my name is Stutter, your Baronship. Billy Stutter,' said the youth nervously. 'M-m-my father is William Stutter of Porzana village and m-m-my m-m-mother is ...'

Bembex cut him short: 'I don't give a hoot who your mother is!' he snapped, waving a knife in the air like a man conducting an orchestra. 'What d'you want?'

'M-M-Mr Stobbins sent m-me sir. I'm his assistant.'

'Sent you? For what? And why d'you keep stammering like that?'

'It's by way of a fam-mi-mily ailm-me-ment, sir. M-m-my father's the same, only with him it's esses, sir, where with m-me it's ems. But we always thank God that it's nothing worse, sir, for instance ...'

'Oh get on with it!' said Bembex irritably. 'What's up?'

Billy took a deep breath. 'It's M-Mr Stobbins, your Baronship; he's out of action!'

'Out of action?' cried Bembex. 'He's never been *in* action as far as I know! Don't tell me!' he added, a tone of sarcasm creeping into his voice, 'it's laryngitis! I knew it'd happen if he didn't give his voice a rest. All that chatter! Yap! yap! yap!'

'No, sir,' said Billy. 'It's not that. He's had a shock, sir.'

Bembex raised an eyebrow. 'A shock? What did he do? Open his mouth and discover there was a tongue inside?'

'Oh no, sir,' said Billy earnestly, settling down to relate the story he had rehearsed on his way to the castle. 'It's like this: early this m-m-morning, M-Mr Stobbins and m-m-me were about our business, just going to start tree-cutting, as per orders, if you will. M-Mr Stobbins said he'd take the first one, and he

squared out in front of this beech. He spat on his hands –
like this, sir – and then, up goes the axe. And you'd think
the next thing would be: "down comes the axe!" But you'd
be wrong! Something seemed to catch the axe on the
upswing and when we looked around, there was this fellow, all dressed in black, about ten feet tall, at least that's
how he seemed, holding the axe by the handle. Alongside
him was this great black hound, huge and slavering it was,
and could swallow a m-man in two bites! Well, sir, he
grabbed the axe out of M-M-Mr Stobbins's hands – the
m-man did, I m-mean, not the hound – and he whirled it
around his head and flung it away into the forest!'

'What!' gasped Bembex. 'Who was he?'

Billy shrugged. 'I don't know, sir.'

'Didn't he say anything? Didn't *you* say anything?'

'No, sir. As for m-m-myself, m-my affliction (thank
God it's nothing worse) sort of got out of control and all
I could do was sort of m-m-mumble in terror, your
Baronship!'

'And what about Stobbins?' said Bembex acidly.
'Surely he wasn't lost for words?'

'M-Mr Stobbins was ready to drop with fright, sir. It
seemed as if he knew who the giant was ...'

'Well?' said Bembex. 'Who was he?'

Billy bent forward and, shading his mouth with his
hand, he whispered: 'M-Mr Stobbins can't say, sir. He's

took to his bed and won't speak – not even to his wife, and he had been known to speak to her quite often before.'

Bembex ground his teeth and stared at the plate in front of him. If he didn't get this situation under control quickly, he was going to be dining on cold mashed potatoes for a lot longer than he had bargained for.

He glared at Billy. 'Well, it's no good standing there!' he barked. 'Get back to work! I must have timber!'

'Back to work, your Baronship?' gasped Billy, twisting his fingers together in an agonised fashion. 'On m-my own? I wouldn't dare!'

Bembex considered. There was nothing for it: if you wanted a job done properly, you'd have to do it yourself! How true those old sayings were! 'Get your axe,' he said at last. 'I'll show you how to cut trees, and I'd like to see anyone try to stop me!'

But just at that moment, Parker appeared in the doorway. 'Excuse me, sir. Mr Scolopax is here to see you.'

'Get rid of him, Parker,' said the Baron irritably. 'Can't you see I'm busy?'

The butler raised one eyebrow. 'He insists that the matter is most urgent and pressing, sir.'

Bembex looked first at Parker, then at Billy Stutter, and sat back in his chair. 'Oh all right,' he said wearily, 'bring him in.'

The butler stood to one side and ushered in the lawyer. Billy Stutter faded into a corner where everyone ignored him.

'Ah, Scolopax!' said Bembex, his voice dripping with sarcasm. 'How delightful! More legacies, is it? More mind-boggling inheritances like this one?'

The lawyer, quite unperturbed, took a seat and said, 'Not exactly, Baron, but there may be something to your advantage in what I have to say.'

'Go on,' said Bembex, 'you begin to interest me.'

'Well, Baron,' began Scolopax, settling himself more comfortably in his chair, 'it has come to my notice that there is, on your estate, an eyrie.'

'What?'

'An eyrie.'

'An eerie what?'

The solicitor sighed. 'No, Baron, you misunderstand. An eyrie is the nest of a bird of prey – in this case, an eagle.'

'Oh!' said Bembex. 'You mean *that* sort of an eyrie. I see. Well? What of it?'

'At this time of year,' explained the lawyer, 'the nest should contain an egg, possibly even two.'

'Egg, eh?' said the Baron. 'Well, I'm all for eggs myself, provided they're properly boiled,' he added, casting a reproachful glance at Parker, 'but I don't see why you should come running out here to tell me there's one in an eagle's nest on the estate. I know we're a bit hard up in the food line, but it hasn't come to that yet!'

Mr Scolopax waited patiently until the Baron had finished. 'If you will allow me to continue, sir?'

'Carry on by all means,' said Bembex airily. 'I wouldn't dream of interrupting you.'

'Thank you, Baron,' returned the lawyer. 'There is, among my acquaintance, a gentleman who happens to be an oologist.'

Bembex waved a hand in the air. 'Why tell me? I know a fellow who's a kleptomaniac. People have these little foibles, they can't help it.'

'An oologist,' said the lawyer severely, 'is a person who makes a study of birds' eggs.'

'Oh?' said Bembex. 'So?'

'This gentleman is willing, Baron, on receipt of an eagle's egg, to deposit to your account the sum of one thousand pounds.'

Bembex stared at the lawyer. For a long moment he said nothing, and then his mouth began to open and close like a fish out of water. Eventually, he found his voice. 'A thouth ... thou ... th ... did you say a thouth ...' He lapsed into stunned silence.

Scolopax nodded. 'A thousand pounds, sir. The egg

must be unhatched, uncracked, and unmarked.'

'But what's he want it for?' gasped Bembex.

'As I said, Baron, he is an oologist. He has a vast collection of birds' eggs, but an eagle's egg is needed to make his collection complete. He has, up until now, been unable to procure one.'

'Tell him it's his!' Bembex almost shouted. 'Tell him to come and get it!'

The lawyer cleared his throat. 'It's not quite as easy as that, Baron. The taking of an egg from any wild bird's nest is an extremely serious matter. If one were caught doing such a thing, the penalty would be severe, especially in the case of such a rare bird as an eagle. The operation will have to be carried out with the utmost secrecy.'

Bembex cocked an eyebrow. 'Secrecy, eh?'

Scolopax leaned back in his chair and placed the tips of his fingers together. 'Utmost secrecy, Baron. I suggest you do the job yourself – alone.'

Bembex grinned. 'Leave it to me, Scolopax. I'll start tomorrow. And for a thousand pounds, I can be very secret indeed!'

Outside the window, a treecreeper had been searching for spiders and the unobtrusive little bird had overheard everything which had been said. Nobody noticed as she fluttered down from the castle wall and flew away into the forest.

CHAPTER 11

A PROPOSITION FOR PUGNAX

Lucifer John McCracken paused outside the door of The Flying Pig and stared up at the sign. 'Hmm,' he murmured, 'I'm not surprised Pugnax came here. That sign probably reminded him of how he used to look in former days.'

He shoved open the door and strode into the bar. Flinging back his cloak, he announced in a loud voice: 'I am Lucifer John McCracken, setter of bones, maker of charms, gatherer of herbs, gazer at stars and caster of spells!'

Three or four villagers, lounging at the bar, paused in their conversation and looked nervously at one another. Then, all at once and without a word, they hopped off their stools and hurried out the door, leaving their drinks unfinished, being careful not to look at the wizard as they went. Lucifer John's reputation was well known in Porzana village.

Mr Fennifeather was standing behind the bar, and as he looked at the wizard, his mouth fell open. 'Lucifer John!' he gulped.

'I believe,' said the wizard imperiously, 'that the

Prince of Porzana is here. Produce him!'

'Produce him?' said Mr Fennifeather faintly.

'Don't repeat what I say!' said Lucifer John. 'You sound like your daughter.'

'Sound like my d ... daughter?' stammered Mr Fennifeather.

Lucifer John glared at him. 'Is Pugnax here or isn't he? And stop worrying. I mean you no harm.'

'Well, sir,' said Mr Fennifeather in a relieved tone, 'there is a creature here who professes to be Prince Pugnax, but he doesn't look exactly like him – I must confess, though, there is a resemblance. He's more in the line of a cockroach, if you take my meaning, not that I have anything against cockroaches – I mean, cockroaches, princes – they're all the same to me!'

'Indeed,' said Lucifer John. 'Kindly show me where he is.'

'Certainly, sir, certainly,' said Mr Fennifeather, stepping out from behind the counter. 'If you'll come this way.'

Opening a little door at the side of the bar, he led the way up a narrow flight of stairs, the wizard following close behind. 'There's one thing I might ask you,' said the landlord over his shoulder. 'It's about our Freddie. We're a bit worried. We haven't laid an eye on her since she went off to see you.'

'Your daughter has gone to the Black Coomb,' Lucifer John informed him. 'Have no fear. She is in good hands.'

'Very well, sir,' said Mr Fennifeather. 'Your word is good enough, I'm sure. Her mother will be relieved to know she's safe.'

At the top of the stairs, Mr Fennifeather paused and pointed at a white door. 'He's in there,' he said. 'Mrs Fennifeather was for throwing him out, but Freddie wouldn't hear of it. She said something about "poor dumb creature" (whoever she meant by that – this fellow certainly isn't dumb) and "saving the forest" or something. Then off she went. Said she was going to find you and get this creature changed into a human being. Sounds like a tall order to me.'

'That will be all, landlord,' said the wizard drily. 'You may go. I wish to speak to him alone.'

'Yes, yes, of course. I'll give you the key. Freddie said to keep him locked up.'

'Lucifer John has no need of keys,' said the wizard, putting his finger against the door, which immediately swung open. Mr Fennifeather gasped, and with a last nervous glance at the wizard, hurried away down the stairs.

Lucifer John strode into the room. Over against the window was a small narrow bed, and on it Pugnax was lying, still garbed in the stolen bathing robe. He looked up and recognised the wizard. Scrambling to his feet, he retreated into a corner, quaking like jelly.

'McCracken!' he said hoarsely. 'What do you want?'

'Stand up straight!' ordered the wizard. 'You look like an aspen tree on a windy day.'

'Do you blame me?' bleated Pugnax. 'The last time we met you turned me into a cockroach!'

'I did no such thing!' said Lucifer John. 'And well you know it! You managed that trick all by yourself. And I'm getting fed up with people accusing me falsely. The very next time it happens, I'm going to make you wear a sign around your neck, saying: "all my own work."'

Pugnax straightened himself up and stared fearfully at the wizard.

'It has come to my attention,' said Lucifer John, 'that Bembex, your nephew, has taken over your estates here in Porzana.'

'And whose fault do you think that is?' said Pugnax sullenly.

'I am not here to apportion blame,' said the wizard. 'I am here to help put matters right. I presume Miss Fennifeather told you she was coming to see me?'

Pugnax nodded. 'She said she would try to find you.'

'She did. And for her sake I have agreed to change you back into ... well, into what you were before.'

Pugnax gasped. 'You mean ...'

'I mean what I say,' said Lucifer John, with a dismissive wave of his hand. 'But things are not quite as simple as you might think. To work the spell we need the shell of a hatched eagle's egg, and the only eagle's egg around here is in an eagle's nest in a tree in Porzana Forest.'

'Well? That's no problem. I know where that nest is. Those eagles have nested there for ages. My father showed me the eyrie years ago.'

The wizard sat down on the edge of the bed and tapped his shoe with his cane. 'We cannot get the shell until the egg hatches, and that will not be for another week.'

Pugnax frowned. 'All right,' he decided. 'I can wait another week.'

'There's more to it than that,' continued the wizard. 'It has come to my attention that Bembex is also seeking an eagle's egg. If he should find the eyrie first, we're lost.'

'Well? Can't you do something? Put a spell on him! Change him into an earwig!'

Lucifer John shook his head. 'Strange as it may seem to you, I am a busy man. I have more things to worry about than you and your estates. But you're idle enough to do something to help yourself. You said you know where the eyrie is. Make it your business to make sure that no-one gets near it until the egg hatches.'

'And if I do,' said Pugnax eagerly, 'you'll turn me back into my right shape?'

'I'm not at all sure,' remarked the wizard, 'that the shape you had *was* a right shape, but if that's what you want ...'

CHAPTER 12

FREDDIE IN THE FOREST

Five days had passed since we left Freddie in Black Donald's cottage in the Black Coomb, and in that space of time a lot had happened to her. For one thing, she had come to realise that she liked living in the forest far more than she had expected. Admittedly she had been frightened when, during her second night in the cottage, an owl outside her window had said loudly and unexpectedly: 'Who-who-who? To-wit, who-who?' She had sat up straight in bed and said in a shaky voice: 'Only me, Freddie Fennifeather!' But she had soon got used to the sounds of the night and it was now a pleasure for her to listen to the churring call of the nightjar and the reeling song of the grasshopper warbler, and, of course, the hooting of the owl.

During the daytime, she walked in the woodland with Black Donald, through leafy glades and shady dells, observing the wild forest creatures and the herbs and flowers which he pointed out to her. Since Donald had frightened off old Mr Stobbins and his assistant, Bembex appeared to have given over all thoughts of tree-felling and it seemed now that all there was to be done was to wait patiently for the eagle's egg to hatch.

Gradually, they began to feel at ease in one another's company and, bit by bit, Freddie found out how her host had come to be living alone in the Black Coomb.

'When I was a boy,' he told her one morning, as they sat on either side of the fire drinking tea, 'I lived in a big town over beyond Porzana. It was a terrible place – no trees, no birds, no butterflies, nothing, in fact, except bells ringing and people shouting and hustle and bustle all day long. And they made me go to school, and sit by a window and do mathematics. I hated it. Then, one day, I lost my parents ...'

'How awful!' put in Freddie. 'What happened to them?'

'Nothing happened to them. I just lost them. You see, they decided I would have to go to a boarding-school. I didn't know what a boarding school was, and I wasn't very happy about it, and I pleaded with them to let me have a day out in the country before I went. They agreed, and they brought me to Porzana Forest for an afternoon. I wandered around, looking at things, and suddenly I saw a squirrel and ran after him, trying to catch him. Of course, he was much too fast for me, but I kept after him for as long as I could until eventually I got worn out. I tried to make my way back to where I'd last seen my parents, but I couldn't find them. I'd lost them! At first I was a bit upset, but I don't think they were really very good parents anyway, and I soon realised that I wouldn't have to go to boarding-school now – or any other school for that matter – so before long I was content. I marched on through the forest and after a while I found my way into the Black Coomb. The first few nights I spent in hollow trees, and then, one day, I happened upon this little cottage.'

'Wasn't there anyone here?' asked Freddie.

Black Donald shook his head. 'No-one. There hadn't been for quite some time, I think. The roof leaked and the door was falling off, but I soon put things to rights and, well, here I am.'

'But didn't anyone ever come to look for you?' asked Freddie. 'Your parents, I mean?'

'They did once,' admitted Black Donald. 'They brought Pharaoh – he was only a puppy. I suppose they thought he might track me or something. And he did, only he ran away from them first!' He stretched out his hand and stroked the dog's head. 'He's been with me ever since.'

'And you don't ever get lonely here, all on your own?'

'But I'm not all on my own. I have Pharaoh, and the wild birds and animals, and there are the trees ...'

'But don't you ever wish for company?' persisted Freddie.

'Company?' repeated Black Donald. 'If by that you mean a lot of people going around chattering their heads off – no, I don't ever wish for that. I've never been very good with people. Maybe I would be,' he added thoughtfully, 'if they didn't always talk so much!'

Freddie turned very red. 'I see,' she said stiffly. 'I'm sorry I asked.'

'Oh!' said Donald quickly. 'I didn't mean ...'

An awkward silence followed. Freddie got to her feet. 'I think I'll take a walk,' she said. 'I need to get out among the trees.'

'The er ... the egg will be hatching in a day or two,' said Donald. 'I expect you'll be on your way then ...'

'The sooner the better!' said Freddie as she went out the door, and immediately wished she hadn't said it. As she set off into the woodland, she plucked an ox-eye daisy and began absently pulling off the petals as she walked. When she realised what she was doing, she flung it angrily to the ground. 'What's wrong with me?' she muttered to herself. 'I feel so mixed up! I wish I'd never set eyes on him!'

But of course, even though she told herself that, she knew in her heart that it wasn't true ...

PART 6

CHAPTER 13

THE EAGLE TREE

The great pine was not the oldest tree in Porzana Forest, but with a height of two hundred and fifty feet, it was undoubtedly the tallest. The first hundred feet or so were completely devoid of branches so that, to all intents and purposes, it was unclimbable. Squirrels, of course, would have found no difficulty in ascending the rough-barked trunk, but they were not so foolhardy as to come anywhere near the vicinity of the eagles' nest which sat, huge and solid, in the topmost branches.

High above the great tree, an eagle soared effortlessly in wide-ranging circles. His far-seeing eye could easily pick out the form of a rabbit at the distance of half a mile, but at this moment he was not on the lookout for prey. Lucifer John's message (which he had received by way of a passing jackdaw) had made him more than usually wary and he now spent the greater part of his time on lookout duty. 'Bembex of Bellonia is seeking an eagle's egg' was the message, and as there was no other eagles' nest in this area it was a safe bet that he was headed here.

His eye fell lovingly on his mate, far below him, sitting tight upon their precious egg, and a great surge of pride went through him. If Bembex came ... well, it would be the worse for him! What a strange race the humans were. What could they possibly want with an eagle's egg?

Far to the east he could see Porzana Castle, its turrets reaching high into the air, its formal gardens and borders now grown wild and its formerly well-kept stonework fallen sadly into disrepair. 'A short-lived people,' the eagle mused, 'but what destruction they can accomplish in their brief lives!' He himself was very old, older than the oldest oak in Porzana Forest, older even than Lucifer John McCracken ...

With the light fading, he spiralled slowly down until he came to rest on the very topmost branch of the great pine. His mate greeted him with a silent glance – they had been together for so long that each knew the other's innermost thoughts, and sounds were unnecessary between them. She settled herself more comfortably on the nest; she would stay awake during the night while he restored himself with sleep.

As the sun finished its lingering goodbye and night fell, neither was aware of a strange, awkward being – nothing more than a shadow, really – in the gathering darkness. It scurried out of the forest, made its way quickly to the base of the great pine and began, slowly and laboriously, to climb up.

CHAPTER 14

BILLY GOES UP IN THE WORLD

Bembex stared up at the nondescript bundle of sticks high above his head in the branches of a tall spruce. Turning to his companion, he scowled. 'I know it's a nest, Stutter, but is it an eagle's nest?' The last one had proved, on examination, to be a squirrel's drey, and the one previous to that had been nothing more than a bunch of mistletoe. The Baron was beginning to regret bringing Billy Stutter with him at all. If he hadn't been skulking in the corner, listening to everything Scolopax had said, Bembex wouldn't have dreamt of confiding in him, but seeing as he now knew the plan, it was better for the Baron to have him where he could make sure he didn't talk to anyone and, besides, he was handy for climbing trees. But they couldn't find the confounded nest! Since breakfast-time they had examined nests of crows, magpies, sparrowhawks, and on one occasion a disturbed long-eared owl had flapped silently out of her nest, turning her head backwards as she went, to stare at the egg-hunters in a most unpleasant way.

'You're supposed to be a country boy, Stutter,' Bembex complained. 'Can't you tell an eagle's nest when you see one?'

'I've never seen one before, your Baronship,' said Billy, 'but I once heard M-M-Mr Stobbins say that they were big.'

'One of Stobbins's longer speeches, I take it,' said Bembex nastily. He glanced up at the dark bundle again. 'Well, get on with it – up you go!'

A spruce is an easy tree to climb, and Billy soon swung himself up through the lower branches and began to clamber up the trunk. As he climbed, twigs and cones came tumbling down, one of which struck Bembex on the nose.

'You clumsy idiot!' cried the Baron. 'Can't you watch what you're doing? You nearly knocked my eye out!'

'I'm sorry, your Baronship,' Billy called out from on

high. 'I'm nearly there!'

'Well, be careful. And if there's an egg in the nest make sure you don't break it.'

Billy pulled himself up into the top branches, pushed aside a few obstructing twigs and peered into the nest. 'No luck, your Baronship!' he called down. 'It's empty, and I'd say by the feathers in it that it belonged to a crow, anyway.'

'Curses!' grated Bembex. 'We're never going to find the blasted thing! Come down. We might just as well go back to cutting trees.'

Billy began his descent, but as he did so, he happened to glance towards the north, and there he saw, soaring high in the sky, a huge bird which he knew could be nothing other than an eagle! He almost lost his grip and fell as he shouted down to Bembex, who was walking to and fro beneath the tree, muttering to himself.

'B-B-Baron! It's ... it's ... it's HIM!'

Bembex looked around him. 'Him?' he echoed. 'Who?'

'HIM-M-M!' cried Billy. 'The eagle! And I can see,' he added, getting even more excited, 'I can see ... there's a great big tree – a pine, I think – and there's something in the top branches ... it's a nest! It must be! It's an eagle tree!'

'What!' cried Bembex in a strangled voice. 'Where?'

'About a m-mile to the north, your Baronship.'

'Come down at once!' roared Bembex. 'What are you doing up there wasting time? Let's get moving!'

CHAPTER 15

EGG-HUNTERS

Freddie walked on through the forest, feeling a little sorry for herself and somewhat bewildered. A week ago, her life had been so simple and straightforward – if a little dull at times – and now, in the space of a few days, everything had changed.

The path she was following was a mere track, worn by the forest deer in their secret comings and goings. Indeed, at one point a small party of hinds crossed in front of her, pausing momentarily to stare with their gentle black eyes before disappearing amongst the trees. A raven flew high overhead, the frou-frou-frou of its wings sounding peculiarly loud against the background silence and, as it passed, it croaked ominously. Beside the little path, the brambles were in flower, and butterflies – peacocks, red admirals and painted ladies – fluttered from one icing-pink blossom to another, probing thirstily for the sweet nectar with their long spider-leg tongues.

But Freddie was blind and deaf to all these sights and sounds. Another picture kept appearing before her eyes and no matter how many times she banished it, it would not be shut out. It was nothing more nor less than the image of Black Donald's face. At last, worn out, she said in a barely audible whisper: 'Oh leave me alone! I don't mean anything to you, so let me be!'

At once, a voice came to her ears which seemed almost to answer her: 'I can't help it!' it cried. Freddie stopped dead. Looking around her, she realised that she had strayed to the edge of the Black Coomb. She had been here before with Black Donald – the eagle tree was only half a mile away. The owner of the voice seemed to be a little way off to the left, hidden by the trees. Then, another voice said, 'You're a fool, Stutter, and nothing short of it!'

Judging by their voices, the two speakers were coming through the forest towards the path, so Freddie stepped off to the right-hand side and concealed herself behind the trunk of a large horse-chestnut tree.

The second speaker continued: 'You saw it, you took a bearing on the direction – north, you said – and now you can't find it! What kind of an idiot are you?'

A moment later, preceded by a great cracking of twigs and much rustling of leaves, there appeared at the

edge of the path the form of Billy Stutter, closely followed by Bembex.

Freddie, peeping cautiously from behind her tree, observed them with a frown. What are they up to? she wondered.

'Here's a path, your Baronship,' said Billy doubtfully, picking bits of twigs out of his hair.

'That would be useful, Stutter, if we were looking for *paths*,' said Bembex, 'but we aren't. We're looking for an eagle's egg, Stutter, and do you know what's going to happen to you if we don't find it?'

'Yes, your Baronship,' said Billy innocently. 'I m-mean no, your Baronship. I m-mean, what, your Baronship?'

Bembex stared up and down the path. 'Let's just say it won't be pleasant, Stutter.' He paused, considering. 'We must have veered a bit to the east,' he said at last, turning to his left. 'We'll go this way. It must be around here somewhere.' And with that, he marched off along the path with Billy in tow.

Freddie stayed hidden until they had disappeared and then came out into the open. Her face had turned as white as a sheet. 'I must get back and tell Donald!' she said to herself. 'And quickly!'

*　*　*

Since the day Pharaoh had run away from Black Donald's parents and come to stay in the Black Coomb, he had never until now seen Black Donald out of sorts. It all seemed to stem from the time they had found the other human – he guessed she was a female – in the forest. Since then, the dog had noted a subtle change in the man. He was continually on edge and the air seemed to tingle around him. Even now, when the newcomer was not present, he sat silently, elbow on knee, chin cupped in hand, his brows drawn together and furrowed.

Pharaoh got up from where he lay, loped across the floor and rested his head in his master's lap. Pricking his ears, he curled his tail into a question mark.

Black Donald looked down, smiled faintly and stroked the black head. 'I don't know what's wrong with me, Pharaoh,' he said quietly. 'It's her. At least I think it is. Until she came, everything was fine. I was happy. Why did she have to come and spoil things? I never felt lonely before, but when she goes away ...'

At that, Pharaoh straightened his tail and barked. Black Donald sighed. 'I know you'll be here, old friend,' he said, 'but it's not quite the same.' He sat pondering for a while, and then, sitting up straight, he struck his hand on his knee and said decisively, 'When she comes back, I'll ask her how she feels. I've nothing to lose.'

Suddenly, without warning, the door burst open and the next second the object of Black Donald's thoughts stood before him, out of breath and looking agitated. 'Quick!' she gasped. 'Come quick!'

Donald jumped to his feet. 'Freddie! I was just ... I want to ask you–'

'There isn't time!' cried Freddie, cutting him short. 'It'll have to wait!'

'But it can't!' objected Donald. 'It's important!'

'Not as important as this! Come on!'

And, with that, Freddie disappeared out through the door. Black Donald stared at Pharaoh, spread his hands, shrugged, and went out after her. Pharaoh followed him, and, for once, couldn't decide whether to curl his tail or straighten it.

PART 7

CHAPTER 16

THE DREAM

Lucifer John sat down wearily under the shade of a large sycamore with his back against the trunk. Having finished all other business in hand, he had decided to pay a visit to the eagle tree in order to see how things were getting on. He had followed the same track as Freddie, but being not quite so sound in wind and limb as our heroine, he had found it necessary to stop for a rest along the way. He had with him his pipe and a pouch of nettle-and-coltsfoot tobacco. Filling the pipe, he settled back with a sigh and began to puff away contentedly.

A few feet above his head, there was a hollow in the tree and a colony of honeybees had made their home in it. Looking up, Lucifer John could see the tiny labourers passing in and out through the little crack which was the gate to their citadel. He could tell by the grey-green bundles they carried in their pollen-baskets that they were drawing their harvest from the bramble flowers, and he made a mental note to call this way later in the year and try to get some of their honey.

Already a little weary from his journey, he found that the droning of the bees had the effect of making him even more sleepy. By and by, his eyes began to close, his head fell forward on his breast and the pipe dropped from his fingers.

And then the dream began.

He dreamt that he was seated somewhere high, looking down on the world. Everything was as normal – the sun was shining, the birds were singing, the corn was ripening in the fields; peace and prosperity reigned. But as he looked, he noticed a hole appearing in the ground, and from out of the hole crawled a creature so loathsome that the wizard shuddered at the sight of it. It had the body of a toad, grey in colour and wart-ridden, while its head was the head of a rat, sharp-toothed and wicked-eyed; its eight hairy legs, long and many-jointed, were those of a nightmare spider and the curled tail of a scorpion completed the hideous picture.

Its mouth was agape and, as it moved across the land, it exhaled a disgusting vapour which polluted everything it touched. In less than no time, the rivers were fouled, the trees shed their leaves, the grass withered, and the birds began to fall stricken from the sky. Even the sun ceased to shine. Everywhere the creature travelled, it left behind it a trail of destruction. Lucifer John looked on aghast as famine and pestilence began to cover the face of the earth.

But then, just when all seemed lost, there came swooping from the sky a young eagle. His plumage was of shining gold and a glint of fire was in his eye. As he swooped, the loathsome creature turned, screamed horribly and tried to duck, but the great talons of the eagle closed on him, head and back, and carried him off. And all at once, the earth was restored. The sun came out again and the birds resumed their singing. A flight of wild duck passed overhead, calling as they went: 'Quack-quack-quack!' But then, strangely, their calls changed from 'Quack-quack!' to: 'Quacken-quacken!' And then to: 'McQuacken-McQuacken!' And from that to: 'McCracken-McCracken!' And with that, Lucifer John awoke with a start. Standing in front of him was his old friend the magpie, repeating over and over: 'McCracken! McCracken! McCracken!'

The wizard stared at the bird. 'Do you do this simply to annoy me?' he demanded. 'Every time I fall asleep, you appear with your infernal clacking tongue and wake me up! I was in the middle of a most important dream ...'

'Dream!' said the magpie scathingly. 'I've got something more important than dreams. Bembex of Bellonia is, at this moment, standing beneath the eagle tree. Not that I care much for eagles,' he continued, 'but seeing as how you told me to keep an eye on things, I thought you might be interested.'

Lucifer John sprang to his feet. 'Bembex?' he cried. 'At the eagle tree? The devil mend him! Quick! We must get moving! The egg in that nest may have even more importance than I imagined. It must hatch at all costs! Lead the way!'

CHAPTER 17

EGG-HUNTERS AGAIN

Bembex was in a foul mood. Having found the right tree at last, it now looked as though it was impossible to climb it without the aid of a rope.

'And why didn't you bring a rope, you clod?' he said bitterly to Billy Stutter.

'But you didn't say anything about a rope, your

Baronship,' protested Billy.

Bembex stared at the tree and then, in a friendly tone, said, 'Now look, Billy, you're an athletic young fellow. It shouldn't be any bother to the likes of you to shin up there ...'

But Billy stepped back. 'I-I couldn't, your Baronship. It's too ... too steep ... too high ... if you get m-m-y m-m-meaning. And there's all them nettles and brambles and briars and so on around the base. If I was to slip and fall into them ... it doesn't bear thinking of, your Baronship. I re-m-m-member once–'

'Shut up!' cried Bembex. 'And let me think.'

He closed his eyes and passed a hand wearily across his forehead. 'Right,' he said at length. 'Here's what we'll do. You hurry off back to the castle and get a rope. I'll wait here.'

Without more ado, Billy struck off and Bembex sat down on a moss-covered stone to await his return. He glanced up at the eyrie high above him and cackled. 'Just think! A thousand pounds just waiting to be picked up. I'll soon make some changes around here once I get my hands on it.' He looked around at the surrounding forest. 'I'll be able to hire plenty of help to cut these trees – proper lumberjacks – I'll get rid of Stobbins, and Stutter too,' he added with a snigger. 'I won't have any more use for him once he's brought the rope!'

With thoughts such as these he whiled away the time until Billy reappeared, staggering under the weight of a large canvas bag.

'You took your time,' complained Bembex. 'What's in the bag?'

'I found a rope ladder in the tool-shed, your Baron-ship,' said Billy, emptying the contents of the bag out on the ground. 'And a lead weight and line.'

'Well done, Stutter! Perhaps you aren't such a clod after all!' said Bembex generously, taking up the lead weight and securing it to one end of the line. It was the work of a moment to hoist it over one of the lower branches, tie the rope ladder to the other end and haul it aloft. 'Now,' said Bembex, 'seeing as how you've made things so easy, I'll take over from here. You'd probably drop the egg if I sent you up. And after all, any fool can climb a rope ladder ...'

CHAPTER 18

LADDERS AND STONES

Freddie burst through the trees, stopped suddenly, stared at the scene before her and clutched Black Donald's arm. 'Donald!' she choked, 'we're too late! He's climbed the tree!'

Bembex had indeed managed to get part of the way up the tree, but it hadn't been as easy as he had thought. Every time he had placed his feet on a rung of the ladder it had swung away from him awkwardly and at one point his foot went all the way through and he had been left hanging upside down, shouting and cursing. But the thought of the thousand pounds had spurred him on and he had eventually got the knack and pulled himself up to the lowest branch. From here on, the tree was climbable, and he sat on the branch resting and congratulating himself on his agility.

He was about to press on when he heard a strangled cry from below. Peering down from his perch, he saw Billy Stutter haring off into the forest, crying, 'It's the giant! It's the giant!'

'What the ...' said Bembex, and stopped short as his eye fell on the little group which was now standing at the base of the tree. A tall fellow dressed in black, a young woman, and a large black dog were all staring up at him.

'Who the devil are you?' he asked.

'Come down!' said Freddie.

'Come down? What d'you mean?'

'Come down at once! You've no right to go near that nest!'

'No right?' said Bembex. 'Of course I've a right. This is my forest! *My* tree, *my* nest, *my* thou ...' he checked himself just in time. He had just remembered that what he was doing was illegal and, on top of that, was supposed to be a secret. 'That is,' he said, 'I mean, it's my ... er ... it's none of your business, so buzz off!'

Black Donald spoke up. 'Are you coming down or will I have to come up and fetch you?'

Bembex considered, then, with a wild sweep, he jerked the rope ladder up from the ground and pulled it up on to the branch with him.

'Go right ahead,' he said smugly, 'if you can! Now if you'll excuse me, I have business to attend to.' And, whistling softly to himself, he continued on his way up through the branches.

Freddie and Black Donald stared at each other. 'What shall we do?' cried Freddie, hopping from one foot to the other with impatience.

Donald knitted his brow and looked around. Walking away a few paces, he stooped and picked up a stone about the size of an apple. 'This'll bring him down,' he said grimly.

'Oh!' gasped Freddie, 'you're not going to throw it at him?'

Black Donald shrugged. 'I can't think of any other way, and we don't have time to argue.'

Bembex, meanwhile, had found his way unexpectedly blocked. Clambering up over a stout limb, he had come upon a large wasps' nest which was hanging from the branch above him. The inhabitants were drifting lazily in and out, taking no notice of anything except their own business, but it would be impossible to climb up past the nest without hitting against it, and then, Bembex knew, all hell would break loose!

Before he had time to decide on the best course of action, a stone whizzed past his ear and struck the nest amidships.

'Look out!' shouted Freddie, as the wasps' nest came tumbling down through the branches, scattering angry wasps in every direction. Bembex, realising what had happened, gazed down in delight as Freddie and Black Donald raced away from the tree as fast as they could, waving their hands around their heads and slapping their necks.

'That's it!' he shouted, spluttering with laughter. 'Buzz off! Bzzz! Bzzz!' He was cut short in his gloating by two wasps who had obviously been away from home and just returned to find their house gone. Bembex didn't wait around to tell them what had happened. He went up the next six feet of tree like a squirrel.

Freddie and Donald peeped out from under the shade of the tree where they had finally shaken off their pursuers. Freddie had been stung on the ear. 'Well!' she said in an exasperated tone, 'that was a brilliant idea, I must say! Now we can't even go near the tree. If you had to throw a stone at him, why didn't you hit him?'

'I wasn't trying to hit him,' said Donald sourly. He had been stung on the nose and was consequently in no mood to bandy words. 'That was a warning shot. How was I to know there was a wasps' nest just above his head?'

'Well, if you'd looked–'

'It's all very well to say that, but–'

'I suggest,' interrupted a voice from behind them, 'that you both stop arguing.'

Looking over their shoulders, they found themselves face-to-face with Lucifer John McCracken.

CHAPTER 19

WASPS AND WIZARDS

The wizard marched forward towards the tree, but stopped at a safe distance from the wasps, who were buzzing angrily around the remains of their ruined nest amongst the nettles and brambles. He watched with a furrowed brow as the Baron of Bellonia continued to make his way steadily upwards through the branches.

'Come down here immediately!' he called.

Bembex paused and stared out through a gap in the pine-needles. 'Certainly not!' he replied. 'And who are you supposed to be?'

'I am Lucifer John McCracken,' said the wizard, 'bone-setter, charm-maker, herb-gatherer, star-gazer, and caster of spells. And I say again: come down here immediately!'

'I won't,' said Bembex stubbornly. 'You don't frighten ... er ... hang on a minute ...' the wizard's name had just rung a bell in his memory, 'didn't you have something to do with my Uncle Puggy? I seem to remember something ... yes, that's it! You're the fellow who's supposed to have turned him into a cockroach!'

'I have never yet turned anyone into a cockroach,' growled the wizard, 'though I have to admit I am sorely tempted right now!'

Bembex took a few moments to digest this statement, and decided in the end that it sounded like a threat. He thought it would be better to tread carefully.

'So ...' he began, 'you *didn't* turn Uncle Puggy into a cockroach?'

'I am not here to discuss either Pugnax or cockroaches,' said Lucifer John impatiently. 'I am here to–'

'It's not that I *mind* your turning him into one,' interrupted Bembex. 'On the contrary, I'm rather pleased about it! Actually, I'd always thought there was something rather cockroachy about old Puggy! You might have noticed that yourself? If you ask me, he's better off–'

'Be quiet!' ordered the wizard. 'You will come down out of that tree this instant or – yowlp!'

Unseen by the old man, a wasp had been flying around him in ever-decreasing circles, and was obviously under the impression that the wizard's head was some kind of mobile wasps' nest. For just at that moment it decided it had had enough fresh air for the time being and flew straight into what it must have considered to be the nest's entrance – Lucifer John's mouth.

Lucifer John spluttered, spat, coughed, retched, hawked, and spluttered again. Then he retired as quickly as he could to the safety of the beech, to examine his tongue to see if it had been stung.

Bembex, having watched the whole event from the safety of his perch, was convulsed with laughter. He had never known that wasps could be so much fun! He looked on in delight as the wizard stuck his tongue out in front of Black Donald, who seemed to be more interested in his own nose, which was swelling up.

'Ah, well,' said the Baron at last, wiping tears from his eyes, 'back to work.'

He looked up, searching for his next foothold, and did not notice that, from around the other side of the trunk, a hand was slowly making its way towards his neck. A skinny, bony hand; a horrible, grey, unhuman hand; a hand you would expect to see on a giant insect, if such a creature would have hands ...

Before he knew what was happening, the long bony fingers had tightened around his throat. Bembex twisted his head back and his hair stood on end as he beheld a frightful, insect-like face leering at him from under a brown hood.

And then a thin voice said, in a ghastly, menacing tone: 'So! You always thought there was something cockroachy about old Puggy, did you?'

* * *

Freddie and Black Donald stared at Lucifer John. Luckily, his tongue had escaped unstung, and he was now smiling faintly as he watched the struggle which had begun high up in the branches of the eagle tree.

'What's going on up there?' asked Freddie.

'There's somebody up there with him!' cried Donald. 'It looks as though they're fighting!'

'Yes, you're right! Wait a minute – I can see him better now – I recognise that cloak: it's ...it's ...'

'It's Pugnax,' supplied Lucifer John.

As if to verify his identity, a cry came from amongst the branches. It was Pugnax's voice: 'Land-grabber!' he shouted, shaking Bembex like a terrier shaking a rat.

'Let go!' choked Bembex, 'you're strangling me!'

'I'll let you go all right,' grated Pugnax, 'as soon as I've twisted your head off!'

Pugnax tightened his grip on the Baron's throat. Just as Bembex was beginning to turn blue, he made a desperate lunge and grabbed Pugnax by his antennae, which were sticking out in front of him, quivering, like two divining rods.

'Lemme go!' roared Pugnax.

'NO! *You* let *me* go!'

'I won't!'

'Right then!' gasped Bembex, and with that he

twisted Pugnax's antennae together and tied them into a knot.

'Stinker!' cried Pugnax.

'Rotter!' returned Bembex.

Pugnax considered his antennae. He would have to do something immediately. A cockroach cannot function properly with his antennae tied in a knot – all his messages get crossed.

'I'll have to let you go,' he said bitterly.

'Well, do,' said Bembex.

'All right, I will.'

The three onlookers gazed in horror as they heard a great rustling of twigs and cracking of branches and then beheld the Baron of Bellonia hurtling head first towards the ground.

'He'll be killed!' gasped Freddie.

But, just as Bembex was about to strike the ground, Lucifer John stepped forward and stretched out his hand.

'By the Seven Stars of the Seven Sisters, HALT!' he commanded. And, to the others' astonishment, the Baron came to an immediate stop two feet above the ground and floated in mid-air.

The wizard remained standing with his hand outstretched while Bembex glared at him.

'Let me down!' ordered the Baron. 'Now!'

'As you wish,' said Lucifer John, withdrawing his hand.

As Billy Stutter had observed, there was a dense growth of nettles and brambles around the base of the tree, and it was into this that Bembex now descended with a flop. As the brambles pricked him and the nettles burned him, he began to make strange hooting noises. He thrashed around, trying to disentangle himself, but that only seemed to get him more stuck, and the hooting noises got louder.

But there was worse to come. If there is one thing to which wasps object, it is having people throw stones at their nest, causing it to fall scores of feet to the ground. In fact there is only one thing in life which makes them more unhappy, and that is having barons fall on them suddenly out of the blue. Since the wasps at the foot of the tree had had both of these things happen to them within the space of less than five minutes, they naturally became upset. They got the idea into their heads that the whole world was against them and they decided that, whatever else might happen, they were going to go down fighting. They soared around angrily, seeking an object on which to vent their spleen.

Not so long ago, the thought had crossed Bembex's mind that wasps were fun. Now he decided that he had been mistaken. Completely entangled in the brambles, he was powerless to escape or to defend himself, and the wasps took advantage of the situation to make their

feelings abundantly clear to him. The hooting noises which Bembex had been making began to change to roars and yelps. It was only when the wasps had got all the pent-up fury out of their systems, and had departed the neighbourhood to seek a new home, that the Baron became quiet.

Freddie, Black Donald and Lucifer John came out cautiously from under the tree and walked across to look at him. He seemed to be composed mostly of bumps and scratches, but his spirit was not subdued.

'Don't just stand there!' he shouted. 'Help me out of here!'

High in the sky, an eagle came into view. As he passed overhead, something fell from his beak and came tumbling down. Bembex jumped as it landed with a light crunch on his head.

'What the–' he said, looking up.

Lucifer John stepped forward and carefully picked up the object. Holding it up, he examined it closely and then held it out to Freddie.

'The shell ...' he said with a smile.

'Of an eagle's egg!' said Freddie, laughing.

CHAPTER 20

A QUESTION FOR FREDDIE

Breakfast was underway in the kitchen of The Flying Pig. Mrs Fennifeather glanced anxiously across the table at her husband, who was busy wrapping himself around a plate of rashers and sausages. She wanted to ask him a question, but was afraid of the answer she was almost sure she would receive. In the end, however, her curiosity got the better of her; she cleared her throat and began: 'Albert?'

Mr Fennifeather glanced up. 'Eh?'

'Albert. You know how I can't stand it when I ask you questions and you repeat things I say?'

'Eh? Repeat things?' said Mr Fennifeather innocently. 'I don't know what you mean. I don't think I repeat things. Do I?'

Mrs Fennifeather sighed. 'Albert, I want to ask you a question. Will you please think carefully and answer without repeating the question?'

'Without repeating the question?' said Mr Fennifeather, his fork half-way to his mouth. 'Why would I repeat the question?'

Mrs Fennifeather passed a hand wearily across her

forehead. She was nearly at the end of her tether. If this type of thing continued, she would seriously have to consider taking a vow of silence. But there was something she had to find out first. She took a deep breath. 'Albert, what's wrong with Aelfreda?'

'Wrong with Aelfreda? I don't know that there's anything wrong with her. What do you see wrong with her?'

'Haven't you noticed that she's off her food? Ever since she came back from her adventures – saving the forest or whatever it was – she hasn't been herself. See how she hasn't come down to breakfast this morning? Has she said anything to you? You know she doesn't tell me anything.'

Mr Fennifeather shrugged. 'She doesn't tell me anything either.' He inserted half a sausage into his mouth and chewed thoughtfully. 'I think she's in love,' he said simply.

'In love?' said Mrs Fennifeather, aghast. 'How could she be in love? She doesn't know anyone to be in love with!'

'That's where you're wrong,' said Mr Fennifeather, pointing at his wife with his fork. 'What about the Prince?'

'Pugnax? That cockroach? She couldn't be in love with him! He's ... he's ... why, he was ugly enough as a cockroach, but since the wizard McCracken translated him into a human being, he's even worse! He should have left him as he was! Since he was reinstated up at the castle he's done nothing except eat!'

'Handsome is as handsome does,' observed Mr Fennifeather, 'that's what I say. When all's said and done, he did turn all that forest into a nature reserve, just as he promised.'

'Only because the wizard McCracken made him do it,' Mrs Fennifeather pointed out. 'And anyway, that wouldn't make Aelfreda fall in love with him.'

Mr Fennifeather winked at his wife across the table. 'What about the castle? What about the grounds? What about the fortune? What about,' he ended, with an even bigger wink, 'the title? Princess Freddie!'

Mrs Fennifeather stared in horror at her husband. 'Albert Fennifeather!' she gasped. 'I can't believe my ears! Do you really believe that Aelfreda – our Aelfreda – would stoop to – would be influenced by–' She was interrupted by a knocking at the door. 'Go and see who that is!' she said testily.

Mr Fennifeather got up and went out to the front door. A moment later he reappeared bearing a letter. 'It was the postman,' he said, scrutinising the envelope. 'It's for Freddie. I'll take it up to her.' He went out into the hall and climbed the stairs.

Two minutes later, Freddie came hurrying down the stairs into the kitchen, the letter in her hand. 'Mother,' she said in a breathless sort of voice, 'I have to go.'

'Go?' repeated Mrs Fennifeather, realising she was slipping into her husband's habit. 'Go where?'

'I can't explain now,' said Freddie, pulling on her coat. 'I'll be in touch!' And with that, and without another word, she disappeared through the door.

Mrs Fennifeather stared after her in amazement. 'What's got into the girl?' Her gaze fell upon the letter, which Freddie had left lying on the table. She reached across, opened the envelope and pulled out the single sheet of paper it contained. On it was drawn in black a large question mark.

'What's this?' she asked, holding the paper up to Mr Fennifeather, who had just appeared in the doorway.

Mr Fennifeather shrugged. 'She just looked at it, laughed, kissed me and ran down the stairs!'

'But where's she gone?'

Mr Fennifeather scratched his head. 'I suppose,' he said, indicating the letter, 'that's some sort of a question. I expect she's gone to answer it ...'

In the early dawn light, Lucifer John McCracken smiled at the scene which was being unfolded in the distance before him. He had climbed into the branches of the great oak which overshadowed his little cottage, and from this vantage point he had a clear view of the country for miles around. The great red orb of the sun was just breaking free of the eastern horizon, and silhouetted against it he could make out three shapes standing on the top of the slope which formed the western side of the Black Coomb. Two figures, one taller than the other, were standing staring into the north, and alongside them was the figure of a dog, his tail standing up straight in the air.

To the north, the wizard could see the topmost branches of the great pine where the eagles had nested for centuries. High above, two shapes circled slowly, watching beneath them. The air was still and the whole world seemed wrapped in silence, as though some event of great importance was about to take place. Somewhere in the forest a blackbird began to whistle, but it was a half-hearted attempt and he quickly lapsed into silence.

On top of the great pine, the eagles' nest stood out starkly against the morning sky, and, slowly, something began to stir upon it. The bulky form of an eaglet raised itself up, looked around, and began to walk awkwardly towards the verge of the nest. There it paused a while, and then, carefully and deliberately, it unfolded two huge wings which it began to flap, slowly at first, and then faster and faster. At last, with a great bound, it leaped from the nest and soared away into the waiting world.